# RON LOVELL

# Danger in Unlikely Places

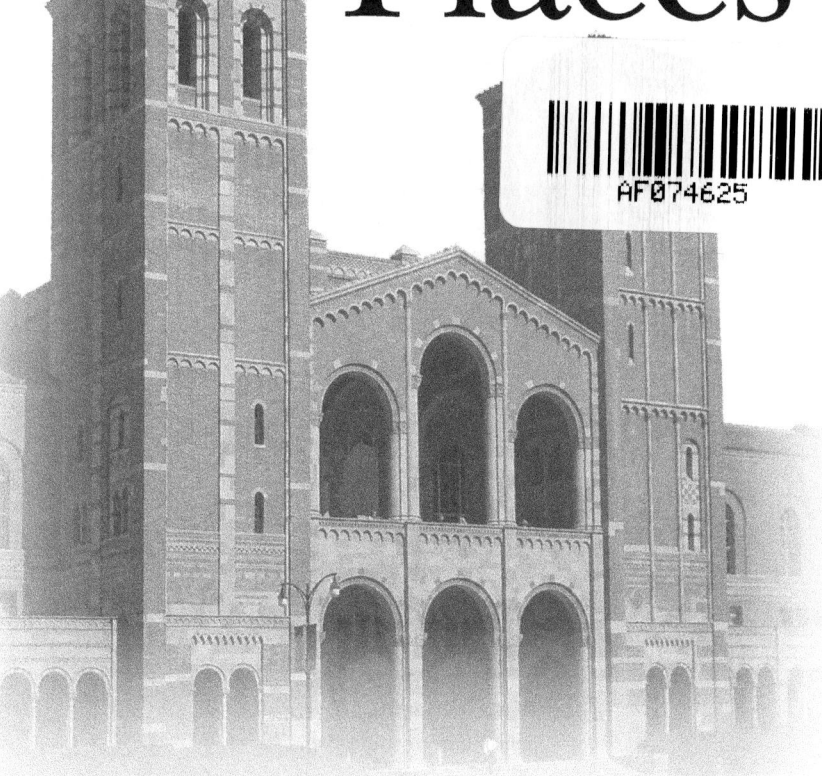

A LORENZO MADRID MYSTERY

FIRST Edition
Penman Productions, Gleneden Beach, Oregon
Copyright © 2015 by Ronald P. Lovell

All rights reserved under International
and Pan-American Copyright Conventions.
No part of this publication may be reproduced, stored in a retrieval system,
or transmitted in any form by any means, electronic, mechanical,
photocopying, recording, or otherwise, except brief extracts for the purpose
of review, without written permission of the publisher.
Published in the United States
by Penman Productions, Gleneden Beach, Oregon.

The events, people, and incidents in this story are the sole product
of the author's imagination. The story is fictional and any resemblance
to individuals living or dead is purely coincidental.

Printed in the United States of America
Library of Congress Control Number: 2015930865
ISBN: 978-1-953517-08-1

Cover designer: Suzanne Fyhrie Parrott
Interior book designer: Liz Kingslien
Editor: Mardelle Kunz
Cover photo credits: Wikimedia Commons, (UCLA, Royce Hall);
Chapter opener photo credits: Yves Rubin (Royce Hall);
iStock.com (evil man)

P.O. Box 400, Gleneden Beach, Oregon 97388
penmanproductions.com

Books in the Thomas Martindale Series

*Murder at Yaquina Head*

*Dead Whales Tell No Tales*

*Lights, Camera, MURDER!*

*Murder Below Zero*

*Searching for Murder*

*Descent into Madness*

*Yaquina White*

*Murder in E-flat Major*

*Murder in the Steens*

*Murder Times Two*

## DEDICATION

*To John Bickerton (1837–1920), my great-grandfather,
Civil War veteran and first writer in the family*

## SPECIAL THANKS

To Liz Kingslien, my designer, and Mardelle Kunz, my editor,
for turning words on a manuscript page into something
readers would enjoy looking at and reading.

To Nick Sharma, my publishing partner,
for the many valuable suggestions he made
during the writing of this book.

And many thanks to
Suzanne Parrott for her designs and friendship.

# CHAPTER 1

**THE LETTER COULD NOT HAVE ARRIVED** at a more opportune—and welcome—time. Lorenzo Madrid read it twice before its essence sunk in.

> *Dear Mr. Madrid—I am writing to ask you to teach a new seminar we are proposing to call "The Law and the Immigration Crisis," or some other title of your choosing. I am familiar with your work in Oregon for indigent Hispanics and also how you have used your fees from high-profile cases to pay for this work. I was thinking about the one where you freed an innocent person from detention under the provisions of the Patriot Act.*
>
> *I think our students need to know how you've built a career in public interest law.*
>
> *I am also asking you to join us because of a policy I initiated after becoming dean last year. Whenever possible, I like to involve our graduates in our work here at the UCLA School of Law. I have taken the liberty of reviewing your*

*record. It is exemplary. Students will be inspired by what you have done since graduation.*

*I am proposing that you teach this seminar for one semester, beginning September 15 and ending December 1. In addition, I hope you will agree to advise some of our students.*

*Your pay is negotiable but will be at the high end of what we pay our adjunct professors. I can also offer free housing—no small thing in an area as expensive as Westwood.*

*I realize that this gives you only one month to make arrangements to get here. I apologize for that, but I have just received the funding to pay for this and other seminars from an anonymous donor.*

*I hope you will agree to join our faculty.*

*Sincerely yours,*
*Carter Askew, Dean*

Lorenzo blinked and rubbed his eyes, then he reread the letter once more while distractedly eating his usual breakfast of coffee and an English muffin.

He carried the cup into the living room and sat down in the chair he had been occupying most days during the month since he had returned from an ordeal that had nearly cost him his life: his kidnapping by members of a drug gang.

Outwardly, he had been brave enough to save two others: Connie, the prostitute who had goaded him into clearing her brother's name in court, and Chito, a young hustler who had been coerced into joining that gang. But having a gun held to your temple and being made to kneel with a hood over your head was not something you got over quickly.

Although he had not sought medical help, he was smart enough to know that he was displaying signs of PTSD: night sweats, difficulty sleeping, and recurring nightmares of the desert where he was held captive.

A book he had read by a trauma scholar had helped him to better understand what was happening to him. It said that PTSD is less an illness than a normal reaction to an abnormal event. The author called the condition "a moral injury . . . a betrayal of what's right in a high-stakes situation by someone who holds power."

Lorenzo's imprisonment and torture by the drug gang could certainly explain how he felt. But this understanding hadn't helped him get over it as quickly as he desired.

He had difficulty concentrating now. He even quit reading the newspaper. After he returned to Salem, he had closed his law practice, quite literally, by locking the front door, paying all outstanding bills, and giving his loyal secretary, Dolores, six months' salary.

And then after a while, he had retreated to his condo—sleeping a lot, eating very little, and drinking more than he ever had in his life, mostly Mexican beer and tequila on the rocks.

His new lifestyle had affected the way he looked, something he barely noticed because he seldom looked in a mirror. Lorenzo had always been movie star handsome with light brown skin, thick black hair, and a slim frame that made everything he wore look good, whether it was jeans and a blue work shirt or the pinstriped suits he wore when he handled the important cases. He took such cases to make money so he could do the pro bono work for undocumented Hispanics that had been his main interest for the past ten years.

Now, his weight loss had made him look gaunt. Some days, when he didn't bother to shave, the stubble made him look like an aging gang member from the East Los Angeles neighborhood he had escaped from long ago. Or worse yet, the henchman of the drug boss he had put out of business.

Lorenzo got up and walked into the bathroom, seeming to ignore the job offer in the letter. As he stared at the face that looked back at him from the mirror, he started to cry. He ripped off his clothes and turned on the shower. He twisted the knob to cold and dropped into the bottom of the tub, his thin legs splayed out in front of him. As he wrapped his arms around his naked body and rocked back and forth, he continued to cry, and then started to shiver as the cold water blasted over him, hitting his body like a thousand pinpricks.

*"Que pasa?"* he moaned. "What is happening to me?"

## CHAPTER 2

"YOU DUMB FUCK," shouted Esteban Perez at the thuggish-looking guy who was serving him breakfast. "I wanted eggs scrambled, not over easy. And I want plenty of hot chilies in there too and some chorizo. *Comprende?*"

"*Sí, mi patrón.*"

Before the man could pick up the plate, Perez threw it against the wall.

"Get me the food I want or you will be on your way back to Sinaloa, or whatever sorry place you came from."

"*Sí, mi patrón.*"

As he waited for his replacement meal, Perez reread a clipping torn from an Oregon newspaper with the headline OREGON ATTORNEY AIDS IN MAJOR DRUG BUST.

"I'll bust your sorry ass," he muttered, as he threw down the paper. "I will feed you to the piranhas." He smiled to himself as he contemplated the demise of the person he blamed for the disruption of a key part of his drug network in the Pacific Northwest. "Your ass is grass, and I don't mean marijuana." He started laughing at his own joke, first a chuckle and then a full-on cackle that turned into coughing.

Then he noticed the man standing in the doorway, holding a plate of food. "What the fuck do you want?" he snarled.

"Your breakfast, *mi patrón*. I hope you like it this time."

"I'm not hungry now, you idiot! Feed it to the dogs!"

# CHAPTER 3

**THE SOUND OF LOUD KNOCKING** on his front door woke Lorenzo. The water was still running full blast and he was still shivering. He scrambled to his feet and turned off the faucet. Then he noticed that the bathtub had overflowed and there was at least an inch of water on the floor. He grabbed a robe and staggered to the door.

"OPEN THE DOOR!" yelled a voice. "YOU'RE FLOODING ME OUT!"

Lorenzo opened the door cautiously and peered out. A young man was standing outside. He looked to be in his early twenties with a friendly face that had, at least temporarily, a frown on it. He was dressed like a student from an upscale college in pressed chinos and an oxford cloth shirt. Not a piercing in evidence.

"What the fuck happened to you?" he said, not unkindly. "You pass out or something? Your bathtub must have overflowed. There's water running down the walls in my place downstairs, and it's messing up the floors. You know wood doesn't take too well to water."

Lorenzo could feel his face turning red. "God, I am so sorry. I fell asleep in the bathtub, if you can believe it. I've haven't been... I've been really sick." Pulling the bathrobe tight around him, he stepped aside and motioned for the man to come in. "Please, sit down," said Lorenzo, running his fingers through his wet hair. "Let me write you a check for the damage."

The young man walked in hesitantly, as if he was worried about what to expect, and sat down. He looked at both Lorenzo and the apartment closely. "You a drug addict or an alcoholic or something? You know what? You remind me of those pretty-boy actors on those Mexican soaps."

Lorenzo sat down at his desk and pulled out his checkbook from a drawer. "No, I'm just a tired attorney who's had more than his share of bad things happen to him recently. What do you think it'll take to pay for the water damage?"

"Shit, I don't know," the man replied. "I don't really need the money. My parents bought this condo for me to stay in while I'm attending Willamette. They've got people to handle stuff like this. Besides, it hasn't been all that bad—I met you." He looked Lorenzo up and down and smiled.

In the old days, this comment and action would have been enough for Lorenzo to want to know this kid better. But he was in no shape now to take on a new relationship, with a man or a woman. His life was way too disorderly for that.

"How about $500?"

The kid shook his head. "That's too much."

"Okay then, $200. Consider it walking around money. You can buy lots of beer with that or take your girlfriend out to dinner."

"Beer I can relate to. But there's no girlfriend. I'm ... I'm more into ... guys ... and studying, of course."

"Good to hear," said Lorenzo. "Private schools cost a lot and you wouldn't want to waste your folks' hard-earned money."

"Not so sure how hard they worked for it," he scoffed. "Both come from wealthy families. Trust funds, trips to Europe, fancy dinner parties, drinking and golf. Nothing I'm all that interested in."

He got up and started walking toward the door, with Lorenzo following close behind. "Chad Dunbar," he said, putting out his hand.

"Lorenzo Madrid."

"Good to meet you," Chad said. "I hope to see you again, maybe around the building or at the gym." He looked at Lorenzo and, slowly taking his hand away, said, "You look like someone who could use a good workout."

Lorenzo looked down at his skinny body and pulled the bathrobe more tightly around himself. "God, yeah, I'm not in very good shape. I'm thin enough, but my muscles have vanished."

"Why not come to the gym with me sometime?"

"Let me think about it. In the meantime, come back for drinks tomorrow at 7. I owe you that much for rescuing me from my own shower."

Chad smiled. "You bet. I'd love to. I'd like to know why you're ..."

"So down and out?" Lorenzo laughed. "That would take longer than one evening, believe me. So, what are you studying at Willamette?"

"Pre-law," said Chad.

"Well, great. I've got lots to tell you."

Chad smiled again and hugged Lorenzo before walking quickly out the door.

"Until tomorrow," said Lorenzo.

"You bet."

Lorenzo closed the door and walked into the bathroom to clean up the mess he had created in there. As he mopped up the water, he began to feel better. The shock of the frigid water and the chance meeting with his downstairs neighbor had somehow changed his view of the world. It was as if the deep sadness had lifted a bit. Life might go on after all, he thought to himself.

Later, as he sat at the kitchen table, eating a peanut butter and jelly sandwich, Lorenzo picked up the dean's letter and read it once more. Then he reached for the phone and punched in the number of the UCLA School of Law.

"Yes, good morning. Dean Askew, please. Lorenzo Madrid calling."

## CHAPTER 4

ESTEBAN PEREZ HAD LONG AGO ABANDONED his cars of choice: older model Chevrolets with no mufflers that sat so low they almost touched the street. He could rev up the engines so they seemed to be growling at anyone who dared to stare at or question him.

Now he had a new status in life: assistant to an important drug lord in charge of transporting his "product"—cocaine, marijuana, some heroin—up and down the I-5 corridor, first from Mexico, then through California to the eager customers in Oregon and Washington. Not that he did any of the actual shipments. He had plenty of men fresh from Mexico and Central America to do that. He was *el jefe*, the chief. They took orders from him. This status meant that he could drive a new Cadillac Escalade—or sit in the back while someone else actually drove the vehicle.

But his status and the whole operation in the Pacific Northwest had been put in jeopardy by the death of his *patrón*, Ernesto Robles, the month before. He had been killed in a shootout with DEA agents at a ranch in a remote part of southeast Oregon.

But he did not blame the DEA for his boss's death as much as the guy who led them to the remote ranch in the first place. It had been easy to find out his name. There had been stories about the incident in the papers at the time. And now he sat in the back seat of his Cadillac, watching the building where this man had his office.

**Lorenzo Madrid, Attorney at Law**—this was the sign in the glass window of the small structure, which looked like it had once been a house.

"Does not look like anybody's home, *patrón*," said the man behind the wheel. "We go or stay?"

"We go when I say we go," Perez said disdainfully, adding under his breath, "Why do they send me these idiots?"

The two sat in the car and continued to watch the building. Eventually Perez asked, "What's your name?"

"Hugo Battista, *patrón*."

"Hugo, go get us some coffee." Perez handed the man a $5 bill. "Got to be a coffee shop over on the main boulevard. Order me a big one and get whatever you want. I'm feeling generous today."

"Do they sell beer in this place, *patrón*?"

Perez put his hand to his head as if he suddenly had a headache. "No, you idiot. It's a fucking coffee shop."

Hugo left and was gone about a half-hour. During that time, Perez thought about his plan of action. Madrid had to pay for what he did to *Señor* Robles, that much was certain. But how to do it without getting caught and in such a way that Madrid would know who had done it and why? He needed to think about all of this and not act too hastily, which was normally against his nature.

Hugo returned with the coffee—one for himself and one for Perez. Just then, the front door of the office opened and a tall man dressed in blue jeans and a blue work shirt stepped out onto the porch. An older woman quickly followed. She was dabbing at her eyes with a handkerchief. The tall man—probably Madrid—bent over to hug her tightly. By rolling down his window, Perez could just barely hear what Madrid was saying to her.

"Thank you for taking such good care of me, Dolores. I wanted to see you one last time to say that I will miss you."

"May God be with you, Lorenzo. Thank you for being so generous. I worry because you will have no one to keep you out of trouble."

Madrid nodded his head. "You're probably right, but I'll manage if I am careful and keep your voice in my head. 'Are you sure you want to do this, Lorenzo? I don't like this person, Lorenzo.' And so on."

Dolores smiled and shook her head. "You're mocking me," she said. "But I had no choice. You have no mother so I had to take over that role."

"And you took to it well, Dolores. But I need to get by on my own." Lorenzo hugged the woman and she walked to her car, still crying.

"You want me to waste them both, *patrón?*" whispered Hugo.

"No, I don't want you to waste them both! Jesus! Why would you even think that—out here in broad daylight with lots of potential witnesses? This isn't some slum in Sinaloa where the police look the other way whenever a crime is being committed. Jesus!"

"*Sorry, patrón,*" Hugo said sheepishly. "I only mean to serve you."

"Well, let me make the decisions about who we waste! Okay?"

The two watched Madrid walk back into his office, leaving the door open.

"We go now?" asked Hugo, eagerly.

"Wait a minute. Let's see what he's doing. I'd rather follow him away from here and maybe see where he lives."

Just then, Lorenzo returned carrying two boxes full of books, which he put in the trunk of a car. He went back in three more times and came out with more boxes.

"This *hombre* reads a lot, *patrón*. Me, I never learned to read."

Why does that not surprise me, thought Perez. "Maybe his law books," he muttered to himself. "Must be leaving town or changing jobs."

"What did you say, *patrón?*"

"Nothing. Drink your coffee and let me think!"

As Madrid started to walk back into his office, a black SUV pulled up and two men got out. One of them shouted to him.

Madrid turned and smiled. "Greg. Great to see you! Come to see me off?"

The two men embraced and they all walked toward the building. Greg stopped at the door and turned around. He looked right at Perez's Cadillac and appeared to be trying to see the license plate.

"Drive, drive, drive!" Perez shouted.

"What, *patrón?* You no want to stay here?"

"Drive, you dumb fuck! Those guys are cops!"

Hugo started the motor and the car sped quickly away, tires screeching and Perez hunching down in the back seat.

## CHAPTER 5

"THOUGHT I SAW SOME SCUMBAGS sitting outside in a big Caddie," said Greg Nettles, as he closed the front door of Lorenzo's office. Greg, a DEA agent, and Lorenzo had been friends since they met during a drug dealer's trial several years ago.

Early in his legal career, Lorenzo had realized that having a federal agent for a friend could be a big help at times. Now he owed his life to Greg, who, with a team of agents, had rescued Lorenzo and the other two hostages a month ago.

The two men could not have been more opposite, both in looks and in temperament. While Lorenzo was good looking and tall and slim, Greg was short and a bit stocky with a red face that was lined like a road map. He also swore a lot.

"Not everyone who drives a Caddie is a criminal, Greg," said Lorenzo.

"I can smell fuckin' douche bags a mile away," Nettles said, as he hugged Lorenzo. "Maybe you're on a hit list or something." Then he laughed loudly and jabbed Lorenzo in the ribs. "How the fuck are you, *amigo*? I hear you're leaving us."

Lorenzo just shrugged his shoulders.

"Damn, I hate that! Whose sorry ass am I gonna save if you aren't around?"

"You'll think of someone, if I know you," Lorenzo said, as he turned to the young man still standing near the door.

"Fuck, where are my goddamn manners?" said Nettles, finally remembering that someone had come in with him. "This is Andy Savich. He's new, and I'm showing him the ropes."

Lorenzo walked over and shook the man's hand, then said, "Sit down, you guys. I just made some fresh coffee."

Greg and Andy walked over to the chairs in the waiting room and sat down. Lorenzo disappeared into the back for a moment, then returned with three cups of steaming coffee and cream and sugar, all on a tray that he put down on the table in front of the chairs.

"Okay, okay, Madrid. What's this all about?" Nettles demanded, as he took several gulps of coffee. "Hot!" He rubbed his mouth as if in pain. "Shit! Gotta add some cream to cool it off!"

Lorenzo sighed. As much as he hated talking about himself in front of strangers, he decided that he needed to fill Greg in on the great changes he was about to make in his life. He owed him that after all Greg had done for him.

"I'm moving to L.A." Lorenzo sat down and continued. "I got an offer I couldn't turn down—teaching a course at the UCLA School of Law."

"Getting the fuck outta here," said Nettles. "Good for you."

"I've shut down my practice for now and referred my clients to other attorneys. I also laid off Dolores, which I really hated to do."

"You sellin' this building too?"

"No, I'll just close it up and decide about selling it later. I might be back, you never know."

"When's this all takin' place?"

"I'm leaving tomorrow. The movers are coming to my place this afternoon, and I'll be out."

It wasn't often that Nettles looked disappointed. He sat there for a few moments, staring at Lorenzo. "Well, fuck, as I always say." Then he smiled. "I'll really miss you, *amigo*." He stood up abruptly, as if to shake off his sadness. "We've gotta get goin'," he said. Savich got up too.

The three walked to the door, with the younger man stepping outside first.

Lorenzo took Nettles by the arm. "Could I have a word, Greg?"

"I'll see you in the car, Andy," Nettles told him.

The young man shook Lorenzo's hand. "Good luck."

"Good to meet you, and thanks for coming by," said Lorenzo, then motioning toward Nettles, said, "This guy will drive you crazy, but you'll learn a lot from him."

Lorenzo pulled Nettles back inside the building. "Listen, my friend, I wanted to thank you."

"For what?"

"For saving my life last month. Things got so hectic, I don't think I ever said that. Also, I wanted to say that I think I'm out of my really black period—I mean, with the drinking and crazy behavior."

"You mean you're not getting wasted and then cruising the seedy parts of town looking to score anymore?"

Lorenzo looked startled at Greg's candor, but he knew his friend too well to be offended. It was Greg Nettles, after all, who had brought him back to reality more than once.

"I won't do that again unless you go with me," laughed Lorenzo. "Deal? I know you're really a pervert under all that macho swagger."

"You found me out, *amigo*. How did you guess?" said Nettles with a big smile on his face. "Well, gotta run. There's got to be bad guys out there somewhere just waiting to be brought to justice." He opened his coat and patted his holster for emphasis.

Lorenzo turned to walk into the building.

"Oh, and Lorenzo?" Nettles said quietly.

"Yes?"

"I don't really think those guys I saw out here before were anything to worry about. As far as I know, we wiped out or jailed all the members of the Robles gang. But watch your back. Maybe it's a good thing you're leaving town."

# Chapter 6

**AFTER FIRST MEETING HIS NEIGHBOR** Chad Dunbar two weeks ago, Lorenzo had not seen him again. They had drinks the next night, but Lorenzo had resisted all the subsequent phone invitations to go out to dinner or a movie or work out in the gym. His life was complicated enough already, so in a phone call a week later he had told Chad about his plans to leave town.

"Wow," the young man had said, "I hoped we could get better acquainted."

Lorenzo had mumbled something about being sorry too.

"You never even got to tell me about the secrets to success in law school," Chad had said.

"Sorry about that," Lorenzo had replied. "All I can say is to study like your life depends on it. With such fierce competition, that could truly be the case."

After he finished closing his office, Lorenzo went home and called Chad with a peace offering. "You were complaining about your computer being down, the last time we talked. How would you like to use mine, at least until you buy a new one?"

"Sure, great! When?"

Lorenzo looked at his watch. "I could bring it down now, if you're free."

"I'm always free for you." Chad laughed and added, "No charge."

Lorenzo ignored the come-on. "I'll be right down." Five minutes later, he was knocking on Chad Dunbar's door.

† † †

Hugo, who had been dozing in an old pickup truck with the words "Cascade Garden Service" on the door, woke up. He squinted at the man standing in the doorway of one of the lower units of Lorenzo's apartment complex. He was carrying a box as he disappeared inside.

Hugo rubbed his eyes and yawned, then he punched in a number on his cell phone.

"*Mi patrón*. I got that guy in my sights. He's mine for the takin'. What you want me to do?" He listened for a moment, then said, "*Sí, mi patrón*. I wipe him out as soon as it gets dark."

Hugo yawned and pulled out a long knife, which glinted in the ray of sun that shined through the windshield. He held it up and ran his fingers gently along the surface of the blade.

"Soon, *mi amigo*," he muttered to himself, and then went back to sleep.

## CHAPTER 7

"SO WHEN ARE YOU GOING to give me the secrets of being a hot-shot lawyer?" asked Chad.

Lorenzo smiled and drank some coffee. "Not sure about the hot-shot part," he said. "I have always tried to do my best at anything I do, so I studied diligently all through school."

"Not my bag," said Chad, chuckling.

"You know," continued Lorenzo, "I had lots of jobs through undergraduate college, even though I had scholarship money. My family worked hard, but they didn't have anything left over to pay my tuition. Nothing was handed to me.... Sorry, I didn't mean to imply that..."

"Yeah, I know. I'm an ungrateful rich kid who sponges off his parents," said Chad, shaking his head. "It's true. I plead guilty, Counselor."

"If you recognize that, you'll be able to rise above it. Look, when you're as old as Methuselah, like me..."

"Who?"

Lorenzo was astonished. "A guy from the Bible. It means someone who is very old and wise," said Lorenzo, smiling.

"I don't think you're old at all, but wise for sure. An old guy doesn't have a body like yours."

"Look, Chad, I told you I'm not going there," said Lorenzo. "Let's get back to the wise part."

"Fair enough," said Chad, looking a bit dejected.

After an awkward silence, Lorenzo continued. "So, the hard work you get. I decided early on in law school to specialize in immigration law. I wanted to help other Hispanics achieve better lives. We have a tough time, maybe not as hard as Blacks, but tough nonetheless."

For the first time, Chad seemed to be listening to Lorenzo.

"Many Hispanics get caught up in the system, even if they were born in this country. And the undocumented who slip over the border? They really have it bad, especially in the last few years. So, I have focused my practice on them."

"I'm impressed," said Chad, a smirk on his face. "Maybe I should aim my future practice at rich kids from the West Hills of Portland who have problems with their trust funds."

Lorenzo got up, his face suddenly red. "I'm going. You're obviously not ready for this talk. When you get over your narcissistic period, give me a call."

"Wait," said Chad, grabbing Lorenzo by the arm. "I'm sorry. My smart mouth always gets me into trouble. I really want to . . ."

"I know, I know," said Lorenzo, angrily. "To get to know me better. That's not going to happen! Good luck with whatever you decide to do with your life. At least you have a working computer now to get on those gay dating sites on the Internet!" With that, he turned and walked quickly out the door.

"Shit. I'm so sorry." Chad was shouting at a closed door, tears streaming down his face. Lorenzo was gone.

Out on the street in the old pickup truck, Hugo stirred slightly but kept sleeping.

※ ※ ※

Chad slept fitfully that night, tossing and turning as he thought about his argument with Lorenzo. Why had he mouthed off? Lorenzo could really help him—by giving him career advice now and maybe by writing a letter of recommendation in the future.

He picked up his watch from the nightstand: 3:15 a.m. "Shit." He closed his eyes and dozed for a while. Fifteen minutes later a noise woke him up. He sat up in bed.

"Is someone there?" Chad hoped Lorenzo had changed his mind. "Don't I wish," he said to himself. He turned over and closed his eyes.

He smelled whoever was there—as a mixture of sweat, beer, and cheap aftershave—before he saw him. Then a big figure completely filled the doorway.

"Who the fuck are you?" Chad said the words in a loud, authoritative voice, but he was feeling far from authoritative.

The figure stepped over to the bed. Before Chad could say anything more, he saw the flash of a knife blade and then the world went black.

Hugo plunged the knife into the young man's throat and, pulling it out, wiped the dripping blood on the bedspread.

"*Hijo de puta!* You killed *Señor* Robles, our *jefe*. Now you have paid your dues, *señor!*"

Hugo crossed himself and walked clumsily out the back door of the condo.

## CHAPTER 8

**THE ONLY THING ON LORENZO'S MIND** early the following morning was making sure he saw the car pull up. Because Salem had no air service, travelers had to make an hour-long trip north to Portland. There were few choices to get to the airport: drive your own car, have a friend drive you, take a shuttle, or hire a service. Lorenzo had given his car to Dolores for her grandson to drive to community college. So he planned to buy or lease a car in L.A., but at first, with housing so near campus, he would participate in an activity rarely seen in Southern California: he would walk to campus.

Lorenzo chose to hire a car service to get to the airport. He knew the company would send a stretch limousine, the kind of car primarily used by wedding parties or kids going to and from their senior proms. The cars were ridiculous—lined with benches on both sides and a wet bar, they were so long you could hardly see the driver when seated on the only conventional seat far in the back. He was glad that no one in the building was awake to see him leave. This was much too ostentatious for a man who liked to dress like a migrant farm worker.

The driver put his two bags in the trunk. Lorenzo had put his furniture and a lot of his books into storage, shipping only some books and his clothes to L.A. He wasn't sure if he would ever come back to Oregon, but he wanted to travel now as unencumbered as possible. He could move everything else down there later.

As the car drove away from the building, he did not look back. He felt strongly that this chapter in his life was ending. He was afraid that without drastic changes, he would slip back into the black abyss that had threatened his life off and on . . . including the episode in the shower a few weeks ago. Because of his preoccupation, Lorenzo did not see the ambulance and police car roll up to the building behind him.

## CHAPTER 9

ESTEBAN PEREZ HAD HOPED for better quarters when he agreed to move from Houston to Portland. The man who took *Señor* Robles's place—someone Perez knew only by his fearsome reputation—had been cordial on the telephone. Fearing a tap, they used fake names and talked only in generalities.

"Mr. Peters, this is Mr. Garber."

"Yes, sir, I have been expecting you to call."

"I wanted you to know that the first shipment of lamps will arrive at your location next Tuesday. We will have a variety of sizes—both floor lamps and table lamps."

Lamps? What kind of *loco* thing is that? Perez thought to himself. "Maps?"

"Lamps. L A M P S. To use to light up a room," said Garber, sounding a bit angry.

Perez could not afford to piss off the new *jefe*. "Of course, of course," said Perez. *"Estúpido mi. Lámparas.* Lamps. That is very good news, Mr. Garber. Is there anything else?"

"Nothing I can think of. *Gracias.*"

"I hope your sales go well." Perez ended the call.

By a prearranged code, the message told him that a shipment of both cocaine (table lamps) and marijuana (floor lamps) had been sent. Some "lamps" would indeed go to a warehouse in the Pearl District of Portland, but the drugs would go to him at the warehouse in Troutdale. Both men were certain that the bogus shipment idea would confuse the DEA agents they suspected were monitoring this and other calls.

Now, all Perez had to do was wait for the goods to arrive. He had set up the distribution plan, using men and women of all ages to drive the "product"—as he called it—to cities in Oregon, Washington, and Idaho, using both interstate highways and back roads.

Sitting in his new office, Perez felt his anger grow as he looked around at the space where he was supposed to work. It looked like a large prison cell, minus the toilet and wash basin in the corner. Horrible furniture, including a desk with a fake wood top and chairs too hard to sit on comfortably. Nothing on the cement block walls either. He was definitely used to better.

Whenever he looked at himself in a mirror, he was pleased with what he saw, as were the many girlfriends he had had over the years. Dark hair, a thick mustache, and penetrating eyes. He worked on getting the right look. If he tilted his head down, his eyes could be very intimidating.

The door opened and Hugo walked in. That was another thing: why had he been sent this goon as his second-in-command? The man could barely tie his shoelaces without help. Alejandro was smart. Even Paco, that maniac who used to work for the *señor*, had some brains.

Hugo slumped into a chair.

"Well?"

Hugo looked up stupidly, as if he did not comprehend what Perez was saying to him.

"Did you do the deed? Did you kill Lorenzo Madrid?"

"Yes, most definitely. I think."

Perez got up and started shouting at Hugo. "YOU THINK? YOU BETTER THE FUCK HAVE! Tell me what you did, step by step."

"I sleep a while in the car and then wake up and sleep again. And then I go to release my water..."

"You mean, piss?" Perez was beside himself with exasperation but only rolled his eyes.

"*Sí, señor*, release my water," said Hugo, touching his crotch with his hand.

"Don't show me!" shouted Perez. "Tell me!"

"I get something to eat at a little market nearby. Very nice *tamales* and *frijoles*."

"And then what happened?" Perez was now resigned to waiting him out.

"I walk up to his place at about two in the early morning, before the rooster crows. I walk around back and see an open window. Nice of *Señor* Lorenzo to leave me a window that was open."

"Yes, yes. Then what happened?"

"I walk up to him as he is sleeping and look down at him."

"AND YOU KILLED HIM, RIGHT?" Perez was screaming now.

Hugo continued, oblivious of Perez's growing anger.

"Seems a bit younger than you said and there was something different about his hair. I thought he was a Mexican like us, with black hair and brown skin."

A funny look came over Perez's face. "He is Mexican like us. What color were his skin and his hair?"

"White like a gringo and blond as a movie star."

Perez let out a shriek that was so loud a flock of pigeons roosting on the roof flew off.

## CHAPTER 10

THE DEAN'S ASSISTANT, A MISS STEIN, picked Lorenzo up at the sprawling Los Angeles International Airport. He saw her as he walked toward the waiting area. She was holding a sign with his name and the words "UCLA School of Law" on it. He remembered when he was in high school, driving his first car to a knoll near the runway to watch for the only jet that came nightly from New York and landed with a whine of its engines. At that age, the idea of being a passenger on that plane represented a look into a glamorous world vastly different from the one he inhabited in the East L.A. barrio where he was born and grew up.

"Welcome to Los Angeles, Mr. Madrid. I am Edith Stein, the dean's executive assistant. He asked me to meet you."

"Thank you so much, Miss Stein. It is good to meet you." He shook her outstretched hand, and they started walking through the vast terminal.

"Baggage claim is below us," she said. "How many do you have?"

"Two. I've had most of my stuff shipped down here."

They walked in silence for a while. She seemed all business and not much for small talk, despite Lorenzo's best efforts and Latin charm.

"I can't remember when anyone picked me up at an airport," he said to break the silence. "No one ever does that anymore, even in Portland."

Silence.

"How long have you been Dean Askew's assistant?"

"Twelve years."

"Oh, great. He must be a good boss."

She looked at him with a withering glance as if to say, "what kind of an idiotic question was that?"

Lorenzo changed the subject. "So, what kind of place will I be living in?"

"All of the residences owned by the university for visiting faculty are only of the highest quality."

"Oh, I am sure of that. I didn't mean . . ."

"Watch your step on the escalator," she said, pointing down at the moving conveyance. "Don't catch your foot in the teeth."

"As a kid, I was always afraid of . . ."

"Your bags should be on carousel 12," she said. "I took the liberty of finding that out while I waited for your plane to land."

"Well, yeah, that's great," said Lorenzo. "I'll go get them."

Luckily for them, Lorenzo's two bags were among the first on the conveyor that moved noisily from the back through the hanging slats. He slung his carry-on bag over his shoulder and then picked up the other two and walked to where she was standing.

"I parked as close as I could," she said. "Over this way."

By this time, Lorenzo had given up the small talk and just walked quietly beside her. They arrived at the car in ten minutes. By that time, his arms felt like they would fall off and both hands were numb.

Miss Stein stopped at a Chevrolet with the university seal on the door. She released the trunk latch, and Lorenzo put the bags inside.

They exchanged only a few remarks on the drive into the city. Lorenzo enjoyed seeing parts of the vast city for the first time in years. The tract houses and ugly chain stores along the freeway sped by in a monotonous whirl. She got off the freeway at the Wilshire exit and turned north along the veteran's cemetery. He could see the tall buildings of Westwood itself, which had been only a village when he enrolled at UCLA as a freshman. Because of these structures and the trees lining the cemetery, he only glimpsed the southernmost buildings of the campus itself.

Miss Stein turned into the labyrinth of streets west of campus, which were lined with houses that he guessed were worth millions. She stopped the car in front of a small, Spanish style house made of stucco, a very popular style of the 1940s.

"This is it," she said, smiling ever so slightly.

"Great," he said enthusiastically, happy to be getting out of the car. "This looks like somewhere I will really enjoy living."

"I hope so, Professor Madrid."

No one had ever called him that, and he liked the sound.

She handed him a set of keys and a folded piece of paper. "The dean is having a small gathering for you and several other new professors at his house tonight at 7. He lives fairly close to here. I have taken the liberty of writing down the directions for you. It will be an easy walk."

Lorenzo grabbed her hand as she started to turn toward the car. "Thanks so much for doing all this for me. I appreciate it. I'm not used to anyone helping me."

A moment passed before she took her hand away. "Well," she said, slightly flustered, "I'll pop the trunk so you can get your bags."

He picked up the bags and smiled one last time. "I hope I'll see you at school."

"I'm sure you will," she said, smiling a bit more broadly this time.

## CHAPTER 11

**EVEN THOUGH IT WAS IN THE SAME NEIGHBORHOOD,** the dean's house was considerably more impressive than the one Lorenzo was staying in. Not that he was complaining. He was very happy where he was. In fact, the house was really a gem of the pre-war style so prevalent in Los Angeles.

Dean Askew's home was huge and very modern looking from the front. It had two stories with balconies and a series of flagstone steps that led up to the front door. Lorenzo suspected that an older house had occupied the lot and had been purchased as what locals called "a tear-down." In other words, the lot was more valuable than the original house.

He rang the bell.

Within seconds, a young man in the white coat of a waiter opened the door. He was dark-skinned like Lorenzo but looked more Native American than Hispanic.

"Name, please."

"Lorenzo Madrid. I'm a new adjunct."

The man, whose name tag identified him as Asa, looked at a printed list.

"Here you are. Great." He put a check mark next to the name and stepped aside, allowing Lorenzo into a large hall with polished tile floors and brightly colored Mexican tapestries adorning the walls.

"Everyone's out in the garden," said Asa, motioning the way to Lorenzo. "I've got to get back to work. Enjoy yourself. Welcome to L.A."

Lorenzo walked down the wide hall and through the open doors. The terrace was large and filled with people holding glasses and talking animatedly. Steps led down to another terrace even larger than the first. On either side, long tables overflowed with platters of food. The bar was just ahead, and Lorenzo walked toward it. Before he got there, a short man wearing a bow tie and a seersucker suit stepped in his way and put out his hand.

"You're Lorenzo Madrid."

"Yes, sir. That's me," he said.

"Carter Askew. So glad you're here. Did Miss Stein get you settled in okay?"

"Very nicely, Dean Askew. I love the house. I really can't thank you . . ."

"Margarita, come meet one of our new adjuncts."

They both turned toward a beautiful woman wearing a dress with a long skirt and a low-cut top that revealed more than the dean probably preferred. A beaded white shawl that accentuated her brown skin set off her outfit.

"My wife, Margarita."

Lorenzo bowed slightly and kissed her hand. She looked at least ten years younger than Askew.

*"Buenas noches, señora."*

Mrs. Askew smiled at Lorenzo and stepped back.

"You did not tell me you were hiring a Latin hunk this year, Carter."

Lorenzo blushed and the dean looked embarrassed.

"We'll talk about your job tomorrow, Lorenzo," he said, propelling his wife away quickly. "Right now, just mingle and meet your new friends."

"I'd stay pretty far away from that one," said a voice behind Lorenzo.

Lorenzo turned to see a man of about fifty, with bushy white hair and a thick mustache.

"George Haller."

They shook hands.

"I teach constitutional law and have for twenty-four years. Askew's my third dean. Can be kind of a stuffed shirt, but he treats the faculty and the students decently. When his wife died several years ago, he went on a sabbatical to Mexico City and returned with that hot tamale. She's a lot for him to handle. I think she wanted security and a green card." Haller looked around. "She's been known to spend some of her nights in, shall we say, the company of others, from both the professorial and the student ranks."

Haller turned and walked away before Lorenzo could reply. He looked around and saw that the bartender was free of other customers.

"Dos Equis, please."

The bartender opened the beer quickly and handed it to him.

Lorenzo walked over to the end of the terrace and gazed out at the city arrayed before him.

"Kinda intimidatin', if you ask me," said a voice.

A large Black woman with dangling earrings and brilliantly white teeth put out her hand. Her dress was skin tight, when maybe it should have been a bit less so. "Etta Mae Bishop. I'm from the University of Alabama. One of the token Blacks at the law school there." She laughed loudly and slapped him on the back.

"Lorenzo Madrid. I'm from Oregon. I was in private practice there."

"So we're two peas in the adjunct pod," she said, laughing hard at her own joke.

Lorenzo smiled. "True."

She stepped back and looked him up and down. "Honey, I'd be happy to be in your pod anytime."

Lorenzo blushed.

"You need to leave this poor man alone, Etta Mae."

Another Black woman had walked over to them. She was considerably more subdued than her flamboyant friend. Her hair was pulled back into a bun, and she was wearing a silk suit.

"Leslie Mason. I'm to blame for bringing this creature here. We've known each other since high school. I escaped the South, but she did not."

If Etta Mae was an acquired taste, Leslie was someone Lorenzo liked immediately.

"Lorenzo Madrid, visiting this semester from Oregon."

"I've read all about you," she said. "Running a practice pro bono to help the people who no one else helps and taking big cases from time to time to earn the money to do so. Very impressive."

"How about you?" asked Lorenzo, looking embarrassed.

"I'm associate dean and also teach a course in corporate law."

"The two of you are getting into lots of heavy stuff," said Etta Mae, grabbing both of them by their arms. "We need to have some fun!"

For the next two hours, Lorenzo and the two ladies went from group to group, with Leslie introducing the other two. The names flew at Lorenzo and although he repeated them aloud each time, he knew he would not remember very many of them in the days ahead.

At one point, the dean took him by the arm and led him to a short man with spiky hair and a goatee that came to a point at the end of his chin. With his tiny wire-rimmed glasses and sharp features, he looked like a character from a play by Chekhov.

"Lorenzo, this is the third new adjunct, Vladimir Volga."

The man stepped forward and clicked his heels. "Like the river. Very pleasing to me to make your acquaintance."

"Vlad will be teaching Soviet law," said the dean.

"Such as it was," he laughed. "Mostly it was Stalin's law, or whichever dumb personage was in charge in the Kremlin."

"I'll leave the two of you to get acquainted," said the dean over his shoulder after casting a worried glance at his wife, who was pulling up her dress in the midst of a circle of ogling men. He scurried over to her and seemed to scold her. She frowned for a moment, then resumed her conversation with her circle of admirers.

"I think he has reason to worry. Am I right?" Volga laughed.

"Maybe so," said Lorenzo. "I'm going to stay far away from her."

"A very perfect idea."

They both emptied their glasses, and Vlad signaled for another drink.

Lorenzo shook his head. "I'm more interested in eating than drinking."

Volga emptied another glass. "Very passable vodka," he said, smacking his lips. "Russians know very much about vodka."

"Be right back," said Lorenzo. He walked over to the food table and filled a plate with some of almost everything. It was authentic Mexican food, a delicacy hard to find in Oregon. He walked back over to Vlad, who was finishing up another shot of vodka.

They stood and talked for about fifteen minutes, about their backgrounds, their plans for teaching, their views of L.A. Vlad's background was similar to Lorenzo's in some respects: parents with no money, a struggle to get an education, a desire to succeed. The difference came in what happened to his family: they died in prison during a crackdown on liberal-thinking academics during the last days of the Soviet era. Vlad had escaped this fate because he was studying in Paris at the time.

"They were both teachers," he said sadly, "so I go into this career because of them."

"I am sorry," said Lorenzo, shaking his head. "They would be very proud of you."

"Sad tales don't belong at parties!" announced Etta Mae, who was still making the rounds. "Come dance with me."

She grabbed Vlad by both arms and led him to an area of the terrace where several couples were dancing. Before long, they were moving in sync to a jazz selection of clarinets and saxophones. She towered over the diminutive Vlad, but neither seemed to care.

"I love her," said Leslie. "She is so uninhibited."

"Always been that way?" Lorenzo asked.

"Always."

They watched the others for a few minutes and talked some more about the school and life in general. Leslie's parents had migrated from the South to Los Angeles when she was ten. Her father was a doctor in Watts, the area of south-central L.A. that was remembered most for the 1963 riots.

"I never really felt deprived because I wasn't," she said. "My parents shielded me from the worst aspects of that neighborhood, and I was sent away to private school. I got both my undergraduate degree and my law degree at Stanford."

"I am impressed. A great university and, I'm sure, a great education."

"You?" she asked.

Lorenzo started to fill her in on his life before remembering that she said she had read about him. "But I think you know all of that," he said. "I hate talking about myself anyway."

"Me too," she laughed. "I am easily bored, especially about myself."

After another fifteen minutes, Lorenzo excused himself. "I'm really tired," he said. "I'd like to get to bed a bit early so I am rested enough to tackle getting my house in some kind of order and thinking about the week ahead."

"I look forward to chatting again," she said, shaking his hand. "Ciao."

Lorenzo made his departure, grabbing several oatmeal cookies as he left the terrace.

## CHAPTER 12

**LORENZO HAPPILY SPENT THE WEEKEND** getting settled into his new home. The rooms were spacious, and there were even floor to ceiling bookshelves in the smallest of the three bedrooms. When his books were delivered, they would liven up that room, which he decided would be his study. The desk was an antique-looking roll-top and the library table sitting next to it would make a great surface to spread out his class materials: lecture notes, research books and printouts, and student assignments to grade.

The only thing missing was a decent lamp. He made a note of that on the yellow legal pad he was carrying around with him. He had already listed the food he wanted to buy at the Trader Joe's he had noticed on his walk back from the dean's house the previous night. On a separate list, he put down the things he had to ask Miss Stein about: if he paid utilities, when garbage was picked up, specifics about the house.

Last, but decidedly not least, was the matter of a car. He had decided to lease one for now, so he spent the morning looking at the car dealer ads in the *Los Angeles Times*. He soon found a

Volkswagen dealership nearby and called to arrange a lease. He had had many Volksies in his life, starting with a used Beetle in college. He now wanted a new Golf GTI, a somewhat sporty car that was a big step up from the used Honda he had been driving. With a modest income and a practice that served the poor, he was never comfortable driving a new or flashy car. Now, in the land where cars were king, a new car appealed to him. Besides, he no longer lived or worked in a slum, as he had most of his life.

It would take a few days for the car to be delivered, so on Monday morning Lorenzo did the unthinkable for a resident of Los Angeles: he walked to campus from his house. Although he would have a new car parked out front eventually, he liked this chance to get exercise and to explore the neighborhood. The upscale houses he passed were beautifully maintained by Mexican gardeners who were hard at work early in the morning. They nodded to him and a few spoke, but always in Spanish.

When he reached a commercial area—with the Trader Joe's, a gas station, and a few other stores lining the street—a group of casual laborers ran toward him and crowded around. Just like hundreds who waited in such places all over town and in many cities around the country, these men hoped to be selected by the contractors who drove by to pick up help who would work cheap—and, sadly, for the men, off the books. Lorenzo knew too well how often such men were taken advantage of. They were usually paid less than promised, had no benefits, and worked long hours. Plus, if they got injured, even seriously, there was no medical insurance. It was modern slavery, and he intended to talk about it in his lectures.

With his obvious Spanish appearance and suit and tie, he must have looked like one such boss, minus the pickup truck.

"*Señor*, pick me!"

"*Patrón*, I am young and strong!"

"Hey, mister. I will work my balls off for you!"

The last words were uttered by a young guy whose arms were covered with tattoos and was wearing the low-slung jeans, hoodie, and backwards baseball cap of a gang member. Several of the others—older and more polite—glared at him and looked back at Lorenzo in embarrassment.

"What do you expect from the youth of today?" said a man of fifty or so, who wore a straw hat, a neatly pressed shirt, and jeans. He leaned closer and whispered, "He's a punk!"

Lorenzo nodded as the other men closed in, chattering at him and holding up green cards. Then he shouted in Spanish and English, "Wait! I'm not in a business that needs your working skills, but I wish I could help you."

Lorenzo thought to himself that every one of these guys could probably use his legal services. The old Lorenzo would have passed out business cards and suggested that they drop by his office. Then Dolores would hear their stories and decide the order he would see them, most serious case first.

The men muttered and stood back, opening a way for him to depart. He wanted to explain. "Listen. I work at the university. I'm just going to work."

Some of the men looked puzzled.

"*Universidad*." He pointed toward the campus, where the big buildings were just visible to the east.

"Oh, *universidad*."

Just then, a voice rose above the din. "*Señor esta un abogado.*"

"*Abogado, abogado.* Lawyer, lawyer," shouted the men, raising their arms again.

Lorenzo sighed and turned toward the man who had shouted. It was Angel Fernandez, the van driver from the Volkswagen dealership who he had met the day before when he made the leasing arrangements. He rushed over and grabbed Lorenzo's hand.

"*Buenos días, Señor* Lorenzo. Good to see you again and so soon. You walkin' and not drivin' that nice new car?"

"Angel, good to see you too. I don't have the car yet, but I needed the exercise anyway. What are you doing here?"

"On my day off, I come here to help my friends get some work. That man you spoke to before . . ." he nodded toward the man in the straw hat, "he's my uncle."

Angel's uncle smiled and walked over to join them. They shook hands. By this time, the others had resumed their chattering. Some pointed toward Lorenzo and gave thumbs-up signs.

Lorenzo took Angel by the arm and moved him away from the crowd. "You really got me in a jam here, Angel," he whispered.

"Jam?" Angel look perplexed.

"*Situación muy complicada.*"

"Oh, *sí, sí. Complicada.*"

"Tell your friends I am sorry that I can't help them. I have a new job that will take a lot of time to learn. Also, I don't have a license to practice law in California. I am only licensed in Oregon. You need permission from the government to practice law in a state."

"Oh yes?" said Angel. "I did not know that. I thought you could help people wherever you are. Maybe you still come to *Oficina Legal,* that legal place I told you about in East L.A. Many of my people are helped there."

"Yeah, I remember," said Lorenzo. "I might do that. Well, it was good to see you, but I've got to get going."

The thought crossed Lorenzo's mind that the clinic might be an ideal place to show his law students later in the semester. It would give them exposure to the real world of immigration law.

Angel turned to the men and, from the few words Lorenzo could pick up, appeared to be explaining his situation. The men listened and then looked at Lorenzo. He waved and started walking down the street toward campus. As he departed, the men began to applaud. He turned briefly and bowed and waved again.

As Lorenzo turned the corner, the punk with the tattoos pulled out a cell phone and punched in a number. He listened and then spoke rapidly.

"The lost is found," he said, before snapping the phone closed.

## CHAPTER 13

**LATER THE SAME DAY,** Lorenzo faced his first class. He was more curious than apprehensive. After all, he had faced rooms full of strangers throughout his career: judges, opposing attorneys, jurors, and spectators. Attorneys spend half their professional lives on stage, albeit in a courtroom and not in front of footlights.

In this case, the audience was very different. With the exception of drug dealers, gang members, and the children of his clients, he had had very little exposure to people of this young age.

He knew that college students could be judgmental and opinionated and easily bored. He had always thought of them as the "whatever" generation. But these were first-year law students. They had to be more serious and dedicated than the lower classmen. He hoped.

Miss Stein had prepared him well. After showing him to his office—a medium-sized room in the basement, with plenty of bookshelves, a desk, a chair, and a library table with four chairs placed around it—she handed him the roster of students and a note on how to find the classroom. He signed for his keys and got a pass that would get him into the building at night and on weekends.

Friends who taught at all levels had given him conflicting advice about the first day. Some said he should make a grand entrance—charge in and slam his lecture notes down on the podium. This would show that he was in charge from the moment they laid eyes on him.

Others said a more gentle approach was best. He should be standing at the door as the students entered to greet them and hand out the course syllabus. This would make him seem approachable and friendly.

He chose the latter technique and arrived in the classroom fifteen minutes before the scheduled starting time to welcome his students to his class. "Hello. Good afternoon. Hi."

Thirty people had registered for LAW 405, "The Law and the Immigration Crisis." They were a blur of unfamiliar names which he hoped, in time, to put with their faces. In his years as an attorney, he had made a special effort to remember names so he could address people in the courtroom, usually without the notes he always kept at the ready on the defense table.

The room filled quickly and a bell rang, like in junior high and high school. He picked up the stack of outlines and walked to the end of each row, handing out the number of copies needed to be passed along. Then he wrote the number and name of the course on the white board behind the podium, hoping at least one of the marking pens had not gone dry.

These were all good time fillers that let him see the students closer up. They seemed equally divided between men and women. He had read that more women than men were attending law school these days—the composition of this class defied that claim. He could count later, but it didn't really matter.

Most of the students were Caucasian, but there were ten Hispanics, three Blacks, and the kid who had been on duty at the dean's cocktail party.

"Hello, Asa," Lorenzo greeted him. "Great to see you again."

"You remembered me," he said, somewhat startled.

Lorenzo walked to the front amid some whispering and heard phrases like "what a hunk" and "he's so cute" and "nice change from the usual old guys." Then he turned to face them.

"Welcome to LAW 405, The Law and the Immigration Crisis. My name is Lorenzo Madrid, and I will be your instructor for the next ten weeks.

"First things first. No cell phones! Period! I want you to consider this classroom as a courtroom. If a phone goes off during a trial, the judge will instruct the bailiff—the man in a brown uniform who carries a gun and keeps order in the courtroom—to escort that person out. I don't have a bailiff on duty here, but I can assure you that I will ask you to leave if I hear any irritating sounds. You are all adults, and I expect you to act that way. The same goes for texting and using your laptops for anything but taking notes. Please refrain from checking your email or surfing the Web to order a new pair of sneakers."

Lorenzo stopped and looked around. He had their attention.

"Okay. Enough of the hard-nosed stuff. I'm pleased to have you in my class. I am new to teaching but not new to the law. Twenty years ago I was sitting where you are sitting. I am a graduate of this law school. It is one of the finest law schools in the country. You are blessed to have the resources—both mental and financial—to be here. When you graduate, you will be among the elite of American attorneys because you got your training here. Of course, you will have to work hard in the meantime.

"I was asked to return to this school to teach this course for two reasons. For years I have dealt with clients who are the victims of the current immigration laws. My clients in Salem, Oregon, are mostly poor people, many of them Hispanic, who ran afoul of the law, often through no fault of their own. It has been my job to help them."

He paused and looked around the room. No one was asleep, and no one appeared to be using an electronic device. A good sign? He was not sure.

"The other reason is obvious: I am Hispanic. Although I was born in East L.A., my family came from Mexico. In those days, it was not so difficult to emigrate here and get a green card. My father came as part of the *Bracero* Program, which brought in skilled workers to help harvest crops in Central and Southern California. They came into this country, worked for the period of the harvest, and went back home. They then had the chance to apply for a green card and, ultimately, citizenship. My father was good with plants, and eventually he bought a nursery in Boyle Heights. My mother helped him, and my sisters and I worked there as kids.

"I am telling you all of this to let you know that I have lived through some of the issues we are going to be covering this semester. Not the tragedy and heartbreak of today's immigrants, but important information for you to know as you evaluate me as your teacher."

He looked around the room.

"But that is enough information about me. Tell me about yourselves. How many of you want to have your own practice?"

Ten hands went up.

"Want to join a large law firm in a big city?"

Fifteen hands went up.

"Work in an inner city legal office to help the poor and disadvantaged?"

Four hands.

"Very interesting combination of career goals." He looked at his watch. "Even though the schedule calls for a few more minutes of class, I'm going to let you go early today, but I'd like the following people to stay after class for a few minutes: Asa Lone Eagle, Cecilia Vega, Brooke Carstairs, Alex Wood, Nathan Chen, Sam Gunther, and Andrea North."

While Lorenzo packed up his notes, he watched the students file out. The seven people whose names he had called stayed in their seats.

"Why don't you all move down to the first row, please," he said.

They quickly did so.

"I called your names because each of you had expressed an interest to someone on the dean's staff about becoming a teaching assistant for this class. Correct?"

They all nodded.

"Great. But my plan is not to have you work like conventional TAs—I mean, by grading papers and meeting students during office hours—but to get you involved in doing research for this class. I have accumulated a lot of written data over many years, but I can always use more. And that is where you come in. I need material to augment the dry written stuff—the studies, the reports, the articles, the cable TV news hyperbole. To do this for me, for all of us, you will need to turn into reporters. I want you to go out in the field to interview the people affected by the immigration policies of the United States."

A hand went up.

"Yes?"

"Cecilia Vega. Could that be people we already know, like family and friends?"

"Absolutely. Even better than talking to strangers." Lorenzo turned to the next student. "Yes?"

"Alex Wood, sir. My people came to this country without worrying about immigration policy. They had no choice in the matter. You dig?"

"I dig. They were slaves."

Lorenzo noticed uncomfortable glances between two of the young ladies, but Wood was unfazed.

"You got **that** right, sir! So I'm wonderin' how will I fit in? I'm used to sticking out like a sore thumb everywhere I go in this school. It would be that way in a Mexican neighborhood, for sure. Some gangbanger..." he turned to Ms. Vega and said, "No offense, miss, but some of your guys are in gangs."

She nodded.

"Some of those guys might think I'm in a Black gang. Yeah, we got our gangs too—just as bad. Anyway, where do I fit in? What do I do to conduct your research for you?"

"Just thinking off the top of my head here, but you might do research in the African American areas of L.A. by interviewing older people who had ancestors who were slaves. And that would make the larger point that immigration—in this case, forced immigration—goes back a long way."

Wood nodded his head in agreement. "Right on."

Lorenzo motioned to another student. "Yes?"

"Nathan Chen, sir. My story is quite different. My grandparents came from China many years ago and became citizens quite easily. The family prospered and here I am now, someone of privilege who does not have to work any jobs after school. Everything is paid by a family trust. I'm very lucky, but I do not say that to brag to my fellow classmates. I am curious about how Chinese and other Asians became American citizens. There were quotas and restrictions—and a lot of prejudice—but that seems to have faded over the years. In its place, we've got today's prejudice against Hispanics and African Americans."

Lorenzo was smiling. This random selection was working very well. These students were practically writing his future lectures.

"And don't forget my people," said the student in the seat on the end. "Asa Long. The roster says Lone Eagle but that just confuses people who expect me to be wearing feathers and a beaded loin cloth."

Everyone laughed.

"Go on," said Lorenzo, also smiling.

"We didn't come in from someplace else like all of your ancestors." He stood up as he gestured toward the others. "I guess it was more like forced relocation. We were here first, man, and the Whites kicked us out and moved us onto reservations in desolate places and kept us down."

"Oh, please," said one of the other girls. "Let's not dredge all of that up. We're not here for a pity party for you and your ancestors."

Lorenzo knew that the speaker was either Brooke Carstairs or Andrea North.

Long's eyes flashed.

"Spoken like a true daughter of the upper class," said Cecilia Vega. "My ancestors were probably your maids and butlers."

"And mine picked the cotton," added Alex Wood.

Lorenzo held up his hands. "Hold on a minute! I love lively discussion, but let's not get personal."

Long sat down and the others stopped chattering.

"This is better than I'd hoped for. You're all from the many different backgrounds that comprise immigration in the U.S., past and present. If you want to be one of my TAs, write a hundred-word essay that tells me the kind of field research you'd like to do and how what you discover could help to solve the immigration problems the U.S. is now facing. Have them on my desk by our next class."

☥ ☥ ☥

Later that night, Lorenzo's cell phone rang.

"Greg! How are you?" He hadn't heard from Greg Nettles, his friend in the DEA, since he left Oregon the week before.

"Lorenzo, how about you? Have you settled into your new life?"

"Yeah. I'm liking my new life a lot. Had my first class today, and it's going to be great fun. Got a nice little house too and leased a car."

"Good, good. Listen, Lorenzo, I've got a question for you. Do you know a young guy named Chad Dunbar?"

"Yeah, but not well. He lived in another condo in my building. Why do you ask?"

"His throat was slit about a week ago. Cleaning lady found him."

## CHAPTER 14

**ESTEBAN PEREZ SAT IN THE DINGY WAREHOUSE** looking out the grime-covered window onto a vacant lot littered with rusting car bodies and discarded refrigerators. This was not the way it was to be when he was put in charge of the cartel's operations in the Pacific Northwest. He was too important to be treated this way by his bosses in Mexico—calling him down to L.A. for a meeting when they should have come to him in Portland.

More than once, he had thought of the old days, when *Señor* Robles had been in charge. And more than once he had cursed the man he blamed for the death of his beloved *jefe*. Someday soon, Lorenzo Madrid would pay for that—big time.

It was late in the afternoon, and he had been waiting for hours when he finally heard the sound of cars driving through the gates. He moved over to the window and wiped some of the grime away with his handkerchief so he could see out better.

Two black SUVs rolled to a stop and two men got out of the first one, guns drawn, then took up positions beside the rear door of the second vehicle.

The man who stepped out of the car was scary looking, even to Perez. He looked to be Indian, but not like the dark-skinned peasants that often became underlings in the gang, like that idiot he had been stuck with, Hugo. Perez had more Spanish blood and had lighter skin and fine features. This guy looked like some kind of tall Aztec god, an appearance accentuated by fine features, light brown skin, and a large tattoo of some kind of jungle cat on one side of his face. He was wearing a long trench coat over his shoulders and carrying a leather hat.

He began shouting orders as soon as his feet touched the ground, and he looked up at the window so quickly that Perez could not pull back in time to avoid the impression that he was spying.

Perez looked around the room to make sure everything was arranged as he had been instructed. There was a long conference table with six chairs arranged around it. Bottles of water and tequila, containers of salt, and bowls of handmade tortillas were placed on the table. The chair at the head of the table was larger than the others, with a high back and arm rests.

He ran quickly down the stairs and walked through the open door into the yard. His new *jefe* ignored his outstretched hand and walked into the building, trailed by the two men with the guns and a shorter, younger man dressed in a suit and tie who was carrying a briefcase.

Perez stepped inside after the entourage had entered.

"Whose idea was it to buy this fuckin' dump?" the new boss snarled. "I keep my dogs in better places than this."

"This was all we could find on such short notice," said Perez.

Perez had always thought of himself as equal to whatever boss he reported to. He never wanted to act like a *peón*, even when he had been in that lowly status years ago.

"Short notice," said the man in a sing-song, mocking tone. "Who the fuck are you?"

The short man stepped forward and whispered in his ear.

"Oh, yeah. I forgot. You're Perez. Our man in the great Northwest. Things have gone to hell up there since Robles died and his whole gang was arrested. How you gonna fix it, Perez?"

"I wonder if you would want to go upstairs and talk. It would be more comfortable for you there," Perez suggested.

The man looked around and narrowed his eyes. "I usually say where we sit and where we talk. *Comprende?*"

"Of course," said Perez.

The man thought for a moment. "Okay. Let's do it!"

He climbed the stairs so quickly that the others stumbled a bit on the rickety steps as they tried to catch up. He got to the top and waited until one of the gun-toting men opened the door for him.

He walked in and waited to have that man take the coat off his shoulders. He spied the drinks and the food and walked over to the table. He poured salt on his hand and licked it, grabbed a bottle of tequila, and took a long gulp.

"My compliments on the quality of the tequila," he said to Perez, smiling for the first time.

"*Gracias.*"

Perez motioned for the man and his assistant to sit down. The man strode to the big chair at the end and waited until one of his men pulled it out for him. He sat and motioned for the others to do the same.

# DANGER IN UNLIKELY PLACES

Perez cleared his throat. He was not used to being intimidated by anyone, but this guy was something else.

"May I ask your name, *señor?*"

"I am called Pantera," said the man. "The panther."

## CHAPTER 15

**LORENZO SAT FOR SEVERAL MINUTES** holding his phone and staring into space.

"Lorenzo. Are you still there?"

"Yeah, I'm here. I'm just trying to process what you told me. Chad Dunbar killed? But why?"

"Maybe a jealous lover—or a former client," said Nettles.

"Former client in what kind of business?"

"He turned tricks on the side."

"God. I knew he was gay, but I didn't realize he was doing it professionally."

"Came from a wealthy family but wanted to earn extra money, I guess," said Nettles. "Did he ever . . ."

"Proposition me?" asked Lorenzo. "Once, but I turned him down."

"That's a relief," said Nettles. "The local cops are looking at a spurned lover scenario. That could lead them anywhere."

"Look, Greg, you know I haven't done anything like that since Scott was killed. I told you that again and again."

"I know. I remember, but I had to ask. What did you and Chad talk about?"

"Mostly his career plans. When he found out that I am an attorney, he asked me all kinds of questions about my professional life. He was pre-law at Willamette."

"What can you tell me about his family?"

"Let's see. Did not get along with his parents, as I recall. They are wealthy. He mentioned the West Hills in Portland."

"Very pricey up there," said Nettles.

"Yeah, the highest. Hinted at a trust fund."

"What else?"

"I got ticked off at him because at one point he seemed to be making fun of the kind of law I practice—I mean, helping poor people navigate the system."

"How'd you meet him?"

"My bathtub overflowed, and the water started dripping off his ceiling. He lived below me."

Lorenzo was too embarrassed to tell Greg the mess he had been in the night Dunbar knocked on his door. In a way, he had Chad Dunbar to thank for jarring him out of the stupor he had been in that night. But no need to go into all of that with Greg Nettles.

"You didn't know your bathtub was overflowing?"

"Long story. Look, Greg, I think I've answered enough of these questions. My flooded bathroom had no bearing on Chad Dunbar's murder."

"Okay, okay. I get it. Sorry. I was just asking about things the police might bring up."

"Why would the Salem police even know anything about me as it relates to him?"

"No reason, if there's no link between the two of you."

"None at all, other than I'd seen him around the building and talked to him maybe twice or three times at most."

"Did he write to you about, you know, wanting to get to know you better?"

"Absolutely not!" It was time to change the subject to something other than him and Chad Dunbar. "When did this happen?"

"A week or so ago, on the second."

"That's the day I left Oregon."

"I didn't realize that. What time did you leave for the airport?"

"About 6 a.m. I had an early flight out of PDX. I arranged for a car service, and that's the time the driver picked me up."

"When did you last see Dunbar?"

"The night before I left. I dropped off my computer—I was lending it to him until he got his fixed. Now that I'm not a suspect..."

"I never said you were, Lorenzo."

"Do the police—or do you—have any theories about who might have killed him?"

"Maybe."

"MAYBE? And you've been yanking my chain all this time? What do you know? Am I a suspect?"

"Neighbors saw a pickup truck parked down the street from the building all the day before," said Nettles, ignoring the question. "Maybe from a gardening service. A Hispanic guy, kind of rough looking, got out from time to time, walked down the street and returned with coffee. He didn't ever seem to be doing any gardening."

"Have the police tried to find him?"

"Not sure."

"That's got to be the killer."

"I think so, but the police want to talk to everyone who lives in the building at this point. That's what led me to call you. I told the detective in charge that I knew you but that you had left town for L.A. before the Dunbar kid was killed. However, they may still contact you."

"Wait a minute!" said Lorenzo. "Why did they call you in the first place? I mean, you're a Fed and with the DEA. You're not in homicide."

"I think it was a reflex thing. Neighbors saw a shady-looking Hispanic and immediately thought 'drug gangbanger'. The police picked that up."

"They called you because they think this killing is drug related? But why Chad Dunbar?"

"A random drug sale gone bad?" said Nettles. "Was he into drugs?"

"Not that I ever saw."

"Did you two swing together?"

"I told you, Greg, I barely knew him. I am old enough to be his older brother or even his father."

"That didn't stop you in the . . ."

"Stop it!" said Lorenzo. "If you are my friend, you will believe me."

"Okay, okay. I do believe you. I was just testing you."

Lorenzo was angry, but this was too serious to let his wounded pride cloud the issue. "Well, did I pass?"

"Just trying to prepare you for what's to come," he said.

"Let me take a wild guess here," Lorenzo said, "and wonder if you think this has anything to do with my kidnapping by the drug gang and the death of Robles. Is that what you're telling me, Greg?"

"I'm afraid it's as plain as the nose on your matinee idol face."

## CHAPTER 16

**PANTERA MOTIONED FOR PEREZ TO SIT** in the chair to his left. The men who came in with him stood against the walls, not bothering to hide the guns in their belts. His assistant, a young man with the face of an angel, sat on his right. He was the only one dressed in a suit and white shirt and tie.

Perez had seen—and dealt with—a lot of bad guys throughout his years in various gangs, but he would cross the street to avoid this crew. They were young and tall and muscular. Their faces and necks and arms were covered with tattoos of every description: eagles, serpents, devil faces, wolves, and black teardrops so close to their eyes that they seemed real. There were also words, in Spanish, rendered in a swirling Gothic style that made them mostly indecipherable, but some that he could read were "Death to all traitors," "Blessed virgin," "My sainted mother is dead," "Pantera is our great leader," and "Pantera lives!"

Perez scanned them quickly, afraid to let Pantera think he was interested. The truth was, this panther guy and his men scared the shit out of him. Perez had never liked to deal in the unpredictable. Since he had been promoted in the Robles organization, he had been the one to make other people squirm. Now, he was the one doing the squirming. And he didn't like it.

Pantera nodded to his assistant, and the young man pulled a folder out of his briefcase.

"Read, Felix."

The young man cleared his throat. "It has come to our attention that the man who caused our Pacific Northwest operation to shut down and . . ."

Pantera grabbed the paper. "Felix, you need to read like you have some *cojones*. This stuff sounds like bullshit. Like it was written by a lawyer."

"*Señor* Pantera," said Felix, "I am a lawyer."

"No shit!" hissed Pantera. He took another shot of tequila and looked at his gang. "That explains a lot!"

With that, Pantera and his entire entourage started laughing. This jeering was at the expense of Felix, and Perez felt sorry for him. How had he allowed himself to be put in such a position? He was no gang member.

"Okay, let's continue," said Pantera. "Your whole operation was shut down by the American *federales,* and your *jefe,* my beloved friend Robles, was killed. Am I correct in what I say here?"

"Yeah, that's what happened," said Perez.

"Show some respect to me and his memory," snapped Pantera. "Say *sí* or yes, not yeah."

Perez felt his face turn red, but he found himself falling into line.

"*Sí, Señor* Pantera."

"Much better," said Pantera, a crooked smile on his face. "So one man seems to have brought our organization to ruin."

Perez nodded, as Pantera scanned the page.

"Let's see . . . I'm looking for a name." He turned to a second page. "Here it is. Lorenzo Madrid. Now tell me who he is and where he is and what you intend to do to him. We always kill our enemies. No survivors! Right, *amigos?*"

The men along the wall nodded their agreement.

"*Venganza!* Revenge!" shouted Pantera.

"*Venganza!*" the men shouted in return.

# CHAPTER 17

**AFTER HE DISCONNECTED THE CALL FROM GREG,** Lorenzo had a knot in his stomach. He had faced adversaries in the courtroom for years, but had never worried about his personal safety because of something he had done as an attorney. Much of the time, he had represented people against one government agency or another. His clients loved him and the government attorneys sometimes became angry at his legal maneuvers, but they considered it part of the game they were all playing.

In big trials—like the hearing for the concert cellist accused of terrorism—the federal prosecutors and FBI agents he faced in court did not like him all that much. But they always accepted the verdict and moved on. And so did he.

This was different, and it didn't even involve a trial. At least not directly. He had defended a Catholic priest against charges of pedophilia, and the priest had been acquitted. Later, one of the young men the priest had molested was arrested when the priest was found dead. After the young man killed himself, his sister had shamed Lorenzo into clearing his name.

In the process, Lorenzo had uncovered a drug dealing and money laundering operation at the priest's seminary. That had attracted the attention of the drug gang running it and brought about his kidnapping. When the DEA raided the remote ranch where he was being held, the so-called kingpin, Ernesto Robles, had been killed. Now, the remnants of his gang apparently blamed Lorenzo and were out to exact their revenge.

Lorenzo shook his head as he cut up vegetables for a salad. He wasn't very hungry but knew he had to eat something. He put the greens in the refrigerator and put a small steak in the oven. He set the timer and put a table mat with a knife, fork, and napkin on the table. Then he opened a bottle of beer and sat down to drink it while he waited for his steak to cook.

What to do? Why had his plans for the future been suddenly sabotaged? And, as often happened, through no fault of his own.

When the timer went off, he took the steak out of the oven and put it on a plate. He got the salad from the refrigerator and put Italian dressing on it.

Lorenzo ate all of the salad but only half of the steak—the knot in his stomach remained. He picked up the plate and bowl and took them over to the sink.

He opened another bottle of beer and walked into the living room to think. He grabbed a yellow legal pad and started making a list.

*Robles dead.*
*Paco, his no. 2, arrested.*
*Gang shut down by DEA.*
*Gang part of bigger enterprise?*

*Mexico?*
*Revenge for Robles?*
*Why blame me?*
*How did they find me in Salem?*
*Guys hanging around office—Greg saw them.*
*Guy in gardening service truck hanging around condos.*
*Why Chad? His drug dealer?*
*Why Chad? Into marijuana but not hard drugs.*
*Thinks Chad Dunbar is me?*

Lorenzo put down the pen and stood up.

"Duh," he said out loud. The gardening guy had been watching the place and somehow decided Chad was me. That's why he slit his throat.

Greg had hinted at this but did not make the direct connection.

Lorenzo remembered going to Chad's apartment the night he was killed to deliver the computer. Obviously, that goon had seen him go in but not when he came out a half-hour later.

"God. Poor kid. Another death on me."

Lorenzo walked to the liquor cabinet that the ever-efficient Miss Stein had stocked with at least twenty different libations. He pulled out a bottle of tequila, opened it, filled a glass, and sat staring at it on the table in front of him.

## CHAPTER 18

"BEFORE WE CONTINUE, I need to clarify something for you," Pantera said to Perez.

"And what is that?" Perez tried not to let his voice show the annoyance he felt toward this guy and that he had to put up with these fuckers.

Pantera nodded to the man who had come in with him and was now leaning against the wall. In an instant, the man stepped behind Perez, pinned his arms, and held a long-bladed knife at his throat.

"Wait!" Perez said in a raspy voice. "What the fuck is going on here? Last I checked, we were on the same side."

A thin smile crossed Pantera's lips, and he nodded again. At that signal, the goon swiped the blade very slightly across Perez's face. It was only a nick, but he started bleeding.

Perez put his hand to his face. "Why the fuck did you do that?"

Pantera smiled again and waved the goon away. He handed Perez a red bandana and said, "The blood won't show on the red."

Perez put the cloth against his cheek and pressed it tightly. "I might need stitches!" he said, trying to hide the rage he felt and the worry about his face. Always vain about his appearance, he hoped the cut would not leave a permanent scar.

Pantera nodded to his assistant, who pulled a large bandage and a bottle of liquid out of his briefcase. He leaned over and dabbed the liquid onto the wound.

"Shit. I'm gonna have a scar on my face!"

Pantera smiled. "I wanted to give you something to remember me by." He turned to the others and said the same thing in Spanish. They all laughed loudly.

"Shit! Shit! Shit! I could have thought of better ways to do that, a whole lot of better ways."

"Calm yourself," said Pantera. "You don't want to say anything to make me really mad. This action was not because I am angry at you. Shit, I barely know you at all. And that is the problem. I don't know you, but I know that you are used to running the things up there in the Great Northwest. Robles was your boss, but Robles—God rest his soul—is *muerto*, dead, no longer with us. You work for me now, my rules, my way. *Comprende?*"

This will never work, thought Perez. I can never take orders from this psychopath.

"So, can we work together or not?" asked Pantera, the same thin smile on his lips. "I need someone to run things up there, someone I trust. I am not quite sold on you, but I will give you, what do they say in this country, a try-out?"

Pantera walked up to Perez. "Just to make it an easier choice, I want to show you something."

The assistant pulled some sheets of paper out of his briefcase and handed them to Perez. They were photos of a well-dressed, attractive woman in her forties. Perez turned white as a proverbial sheet.

Pantera smiled again. "A good likeness, don't you think? You have a beautiful sister."

※ ※ ※

Later that night, a telephone rang in the dressing room of a fancy house in Westwood, near the UCLA campus.

"Rita, it's your brother!" said the voice at the other end.

"I told you never to call me here or anywhere," Margarita Askew hissed. "You are dead to..."

"You will be really dead if you don't listen to..."

"Shut up! Shut up!" she said in a loud whisper. "You need to leave me alone. I have a whole new life now!"

"Stop talking and listen, for once in your life," he said. "Someone bad may be after you. I cannot protect you this time, only warn you. And I just did that."

The phone went dead on the other end, and she stood looking at it for several seconds.

"Darling," said a voice from the other room. "Were you talking to someone? Come to bed."

## CHAPTER 19

**LORENZO PREPARED HIS FIRST LECTURE** in the same way he got ready for trial: he jotted down the points he wanted to make on several 3 x 5 cards. Reading from a prepared lecture was not his style—much too rigid and formal. It also made him seem ill-prepared. If you had to look at the pages in front of you to make your points, he thought, you might not know your subject well enough to be teaching the course in the first place.

This time he was already standing at the lectern when the students filed into the room. He nodded to each of them, asking the seven TAs to stay behind after class ended.

"Immigration law in the United States got a lot more important in 2013 and 2014 for two reasons. Who can tell me what those are?"

Four hands went up.

"Yes . . ." he consulted the class roster, "Peter."

"The upcoming off-year elections."

"Well, in part. But that isn't the whole reason. Yes . . . Veronica."

"Because the president is African American, and he wants to help other people of color."

"Yes! One more thought? Nathan." He was glad that one of his TAs was willing to try an answer.

"Because immigration is a hot-button issue, and both political parties want to get the votes of Hispanics."

"Bingo, Nathan! Yes. So you were part right, Peter. The president was reelected because of the large numbers of Hispanics and African Americans who voted for him. The Republicans lost much of that vote, and they have been trying ever since to figure out a way to tap into it."

He looked around and focused on another of his TAs. "Cecilia."

"Yes, sir?"

"What other issue has been dominant?"

"All those little kids from El Salvador, Honduras, and Guatemala being afraid of the drug gangs?"

"That's it. These kids, many of them not even in their teens yet, want to rejoin family members up here to get away from the poverty, degradation, and death of the countries they live in.

"During the first few months of 2014, thousands of them flooded the border. They risked death from the *coyotes* their families paid to sneak them in or from the heat of the deserts and the dangerous rivers they had to cross. Some got through and were reunited with their families. Many wound up in detention centers along the Mexican border.

"Because of the law that all illegals must have a court hearing before they are deported, the immigration courts in many American cities have been overwhelmed. By September 2014, the number of cases pending in immigration courts had reached 375,000. Incredible? But very true.

"An even sadder part of this story involves the lack of personnel, both to process the cases in court and to represent the kids when they go to court. Without an attorney, the young migrants are doomed to deportation."

Lorenzo continued with a summary of the current situation, then gave a brief history of the various groups of immigrants who had come to the United States since the beginning of the twentieth century: the Irish, Eastern Europeans, Germans, and Chinese.

"As an interesting and tragic side note, let's not forget the African Americans who were brought here as slaves and the Native Americans who were already here and were first nearly obliterated and then forcibly moved to reservations. The tide of immigrants has always swept over this country to a point, at times, where it seemed on the verge of overwhelming us."

He gave his students their first assignments: prepare research papers on immigration cases from the early twentieth century, and write a summary and an analysis of the final outcome. Their reports would be due in a week. In the meantime, he planned to take his TAs to East L.A. for some field research.

Of the seven students who had expressed an interest in becoming TAs, only four stayed after class: Asa Lone Eagle, Cecilia Vega, Alex Wood, and Nathan Chen. The others passed notes to him as they exited class, pleading busy schedules. Four would do fine, Lorenzo thought to himself, especially if the four were dedicated and smart.

## CHAPTER 20

**BEFORE HE TOOK HIS STUDENTS TO EAST L.A.,** Lorenzo needed to go there himself, both to assess how dangerous it was and to try to find neighborhood people who might help him. Although he had grown up there, that was thirty years ago, before murderous drug gangs and desperate migrants from Central America arrived on the scene. He dressed like a local—with his blue work shirt, jeans, and straw hat, he might pass for one of the men hanging out on street corners, hoping to get a day's worth of work. He also rented a beat-up junker from a used car dealer on Olympic Boulevard. His new VW would attract too much attention.

To his surprise, the neighborhood had not changed as much as he had thought it would have. Street after street was lined with houses and apartment buildings made of stucco, probably dating from the 1930s and 1940s. Some had well-kept lawns lined with flowers; others, however, had rusting car bodies and abandoned freezers in the front yards.

He drove by the house where he grew up, which was right next to the nursery his father had owned and where he and his sisters had worked all through school. The windows of the house were boarded up and many in the nursery building were broken. The large lot behind the nursery, where his father had grown many of the plants he sold in the store, was covered with waist-high weeds.

Lorenzo fought back tears as he remembered the event that had changed his life and had driven him from this place and his family forever.

## LORENZO MADRID'S STORY

*While he was at UCLA as an undergraduate, Lorenzo Madrid had met Scott Henshaw, an Anglo as different from himself as anyone could be. Scott came from a wealthy family and had grown up just over the hill from East L.A. in Pasadena. He was majoring in sociology and psychology, with plans to go into social work in the very kind of neighborhood that Lorenzo had been born into. From the start, Scott was interested in Lorenzo's childhood, from a professional point of view.*

*After a month or so of late-night chats, Lorenzo and Scott became lovers. Lorenzo had never been happier. After years of hiding his homosexuality in the macho Hispanic culture, he could finally be himself and not pretend that he liked girls.*

*After six months, he was spending most of his time with Scott when he wasn't in class. At about that time, he went home for a visit. One morning at breakfast, his mother sensed he was not happy. She asked him if he had a special friend, and he told her about Scott. She took the* news fairly well, but wondered out loud how his father would react.

While they were talking, his father walked into the room. "React to what?" he had asked.

Lorenzo told him about Scott. His father got so angry that he hit Lorenzo hard enough to knock him over. His words were searing. "No son of mine is going to be a fairy!" he yelled. He was so upset, in fact, that he had a heart attack while standing over Lorenzo.

They rushed him to the hospital, and he was in critical condition for a week. After he was well enough to come home, it became clear to Lorenzo that his father would never be able to run the nursery again. So Lorenzo dropped out of school for the rest of that year and moved back home. He and his father never spoke of it again.

Lorenzo was miserable. No studies, no sense of accomplishment, no Scott. He did not see Scott during this period, although they secretly talked on the phone nearly every day.

After two months, Scott decided to visit Lorenzo at the nursery. Lorenzo warned him about coming into East L.A. with his white skin and blond hair and expensive convertible. He worried that he would instantly be a target.

Lorenzo told his mother he would be staying late to work on the books. Scott arrived about 9 p.m., and they embraced immediately. He showed Scott around, and they settled down on the sagging couch in the office. Just as they were beginning to take off their clothes, Lorenzo heard a noise in the store and sat up. Enrique, the kid who worked at the nursery after school, had come back to pick up a school book. He saw the two of them, half-dressed, and immediately guessed what was about to go happen.

Later, when he could think rationally about what did happen, Lorenzo decided that Enrique was not a bad kid. But he was a gang wannabe and his shouts of maricón that night brought a lot of real gangbangers rushing into the building.

The leader of the pack—a tall, skinny, nasty punk named Eduardo, with tattoos all over his upper body—walked over and started laughing at Lorenzo and Scott. Then he and the others started kicking both of them with their steel-toed boots. Soon, however, they concentrated on Scott, probably because he was a pretty-boy gringo.

They dragged Lorenzo away from Scott and sat him up against the doorway. Then they tore off Scott's clothes and began to cut him. Lorenzo tried to yell but one of the gangbangers stuffed a T-shirt in his mouth. He could feel blood running down his face and his chest. After several minutes, Scott fainted and then they started spitting on him.

When it was over, Eduardo walked over to Lorenzo. "You're a disgrace to Mexico," he shouted. "There's no place for a maricón in our culture."

He did not hit Lorenzo again. At his signal, all the men left the room.

Lorenzo wiped the blood off his face and staggered over to where Scott lay. He rubbed his face and his arms, but got no response. He lifted his arm and could not find a pulse. Scott was dead.

All these years later, Lorenzo still got emotional when he thought about this, which he seldom did.

"Time to move on," he muttered, wiping his eyes.

He picked up a piece of paper from the seat next to him. He had jotted down the name of the legal clinic that Angel, the guy from the car dealership, had mentioned. *Oficina Legal.* He had looked up the address and figured out its location. If he wasn't mistaken, it was only five blocks away.

## CHAPTER 21

**THE BANDAGE PANTERA'S GOON HAD GIVEN HIM** did little to stop the bleeding, so Perez ran to the bathroom and used the mirror to check his face. Taking out his own handkerchief, he pressed it against the wound. When he returned to the conference room, he flashed an angry look at Pantera, but said nothing.

"I guess my little calling card went a bit too deep, eh *compadre?*"

The other men laughed.

"I asked you a question!"

How could he respond without showing his hatred or appearing to grovel. "I've had worse things happen to me," said Perez. "Now tell me why you have photos of my sister, please *señor.*" Perez had not had to plead since he was young and new to the Robles gang. He calculated that a changed tone in his voice might distract Pantera enough to get on with business and get out of here.

Pantera picked up the photos, struck a match, and watched them slowly disintegrate.

"Your sister means nothing to me," he said disdainfully. "I once had a family too, but I don't even know where they are now. A man in my position cannot afford to have anyone dear to him. I bed whores for a few nights and let them go on to one of my men. You know I am, as some women have said, very well endowed." He smiled at the thought. "By the way, anytime you want a good piece of brown ass, let me know."

"Sure, sure," said Perez. "With all due respect, I believe we have more important things to talk about, right *el jefe?*"

Pantera frowned and took another swig of tequila. "As a rule, I decide what we talk about, but I guess you're right." More tequila. He pushed the bottle toward Perez. "Have some yourself, but wipe your mouth before you drink. I'm careful about my health."

"No, *muchas gracias, señor*," said Perez. "I need a clear head to keep up with you."

Pantera laughed. "Glad we understand each other. Now we can get down to business." He picked up some sheets of paper and squinted at the words.

The great panther can't see very well, thought Perez, or maybe he can't read.

"Read this shit for me, Felix," he shouted at his buttoned-down assistant. "That's why I have people like you around. I don't need to strain my eyes. They need to be ready to focus on my prey."

This guy is really nuts, thought Perez. I am working for a total psychopath.

Felix cleared his throat and read out loud, "Lorenzo Madrid is an attorney of Hispanic descent who usually practices law in Salem, Oregon. For many years, he has handled the cases of the undocumented who come to America to create a better life and to..."

"Get away from fuckers like me," shouted Pantera. "I want the kids to be in gangs and the parents to pay for protection. They are all weaklings...." Pantera took two swigs from the bottle. "And I love weaklings. Why? 'Cause they're so easy to control!" Pantera swirled the bottle again but did not drink from it. "And who gets them here?" He pounded his chest. "I do, or my *coyotes* do. And I get paid so they can escape from me."

Pantera turned and looked straight into Perez's eyes. "And then I find them and make them pay more."

Pantera laughed so hard that he began to cough. He waved Felix away when he offered him a glass of water. He took another drink of tequila and nodded to Felix to continue.

"Last year, he discovered the arrangement between *Señor* Robles and a Catholic priest in Oregon who helped the *señor* smuggle drugs into the Pacific Northwest and handle the money derived from those drugs."

Pantera put up his hand. *"Como se dice.* Derived?"

"They **made** money from selling the drugs," answered Felix.

"Oh yes, of course," said Pantera. "Why the fuck didn't you say it that way?" A look of sheepishness crossed his face for a second, before it hardened again. "Go on, go on."

Felix continued. "The lawyer was kidnapped along with a woman and taken to a ranch that *Señor* Robles owned in the deserts of Oregon."

Pantera held up his hand. "I thought it only rained in Oregon."

"There is an eastern half that is very dry all the time, and there is even a desert," Perez said. "I've seen it myself."

Pantera shook his head. "Hard to believe. Go on, Felix."

"The lawyer had a friend in the DEA who knew about *Señor* Robles's operation, and he raided the ranch to set free his friend—this man Madrid—and arrest the *señor*. There was a gunfight, and *Señor* Robles was killed. All his men were arrested and the drug organization was shut down."

Pantera turned to Perez. "You knew of this?"

"Yes, but I was down here in L.A. keeping things going while *Señor* Robles was away. I only heard about what happened later when..."

"When it was too late to save your *jefe*."

Perez held his tongue and nodded in agreement.

"So we must get our revenge on this man Madrid," said Pantera. "He must die for what he did to poor *Señor* Robles and to our whole setup. We make too much money up there to let it stay closed for very long. We're losing money we could be making."

Perez nodded. If you would just let me handle this, he thought, it would be taken care of. I don't need you and your boys to push into my business. But he couldn't say this out loud. Pantera was much too unpredictable for that.

"Now, tell me how you failed to have him killed in Oregon," Pantera demanded.

Perez continued. "We waited outside his office and then we..."

"Who is this **we**?"

"Myself and a man named Hugo, who had been *Señor* Robles's bodyguard," said Perez. "He was sent from here to Oregon to assist me. At my instruction, he followed Madrid to his home and waited for the chance to kill him. One night he waited outside the building and then went in and slit his throat. Only..."

"He killed the wrong man," said Pantera. "And you don't know where the fuck the real Madrid is."

The panther was very well informed. Perez was not sure how he knew what he knew, but he obviously had good sources in the gang.

"We think he moved here to L.A., but we're not sure where."

"Where is this man Hugo?"

"I guess he is outside. He works out of this office and does what I tell him to do."

Pantera summoned one of his men, who bent down to hear what he had to say, then walked out the door. Pantera sat quietly, tapping his fingers on the table. In a few minutes, the man returned with Hugo, who walked over to Pantera and bowed slightly.

"It is a distinct honor to meet you, *el jefe*," he said with a smile.

"Sit down. It is not so nice to meet the imbecile who fucked up the first big job he was given."

Hugo looked confused. "Fucked up, *el jefe?*"

"Messed up. Screwed up. *Eres estúpido!*"

Hugo sat down.

"Look at me!" shouted Pantera. He nodded to one of his men who walked up behind Hugo and slashed his throat so deeply that the blood sprayed out across the table and onto both Felix and Perez. Pantera got up and walked over to Hugo. He put a hand under his chin and stared into his eyes until they became lifeless.

"Idiots, all of you! I am cursed to have to deal with idiots!"

He looked at Perez, as one of the men dragged Hugo's body out of the room, leaving a trail of blood behind it. "I am hoping that you aren't an idiot, *Señor* Perez. But I guess only time will provide me with that answer."

"Clean up this blood!" Pantera yelled at the other man, holding out his hand so that his man could wipe away the blood.

## CHAPTER 22

**THE BUILDING STOOD OUT** from the other structures on the street because it looked as if it had been freshly painted. It resembled Lorenzo's office in Salem, although it was larger. He parked down the street and walked up the steps onto a porch. He paused to read the sign on the door.

> ***OFICINA LEGAL***
> **Victoria Ramos**
> **Ronaldo Soto**
> ***Entre por favor.***

As he walked in, he saw that the room was filled with Hispanics of all ages and descriptions—older men and women with worried looks on their faces clutching files; younger women with several children sitting beside them or on the floor playing with toys. Many of these young women held tiny babies. A few single men, most dressed like him in jeans and work shirts and straw hats, stood along the far wall. Lorenzo might well have been in his Salem office.

"Yes. May I help you, *señor?*" The woman behind the front counter might well have been his secretary, Dolores, but she was younger.

"I want to see whoever is in charge," he said.

"And so do all these other people. Do you have an appointment?"

"No, I don't."

"Well, both attorneys are very busy today, as you can see." She gestured toward the people in the room.

"I don't need a lawyer. I . . ."

"Well then, why are you here? We have no time for people who do not have legal problems."

This was going to be tough, thought Lorenzo. He did not want to say who he really was and what he wanted with so many others listening. He leaned closer to the woman, who seemed to recoil.

"Please. Stand back. I can hear you!"

"I really just wanted to make an appointment on a non-legal matter."

"We deal only with legal problems here. Social services are dealt with by the government. State or city? Do you need financial help? Are you in trouble?"

By now all eyes in the room were on Lorenzo. Who was this *peón*, and why was she asking him so many questions?

Lorenzo stood there for a moment and was about to turn around and walk out the door when he became aware of someone standing in the doorway at the back of the room.

"Is there a problem, Gloriana? You were talking rather loudly, and I could hear you in the back."

"Sorry, Victoria. But this man was making a pest of himself."

The person standing in the doorway was one of the most beautiful women Lorenzo had ever seen. Her black hair was pulled back in a bun and held in place by a turquoise barrette. She was dressed in a blue blouse and skin-tight jeans that accentuated her slim figure. She had tucked the jeans into the tops of her boots. Tortoiseshell glasses were perched on the top of her head, which, with the hairstyle, made her look like a librarian—a very sexy librarian.

"Can I help? *Habla Español?*"

Her beauty left Lorenzo speechless for a moment, something that seldom happened to him. He nodded. "Yes, but I speak English better than I do Spanish." He stepped over to her and said, "A word in private, please?"

Much to the chagrin of Gloriana, she motioned him inside the door.

"*Un momento, por favor,*" she said to the people in the outer office. Then she looked at Lorenzo.

"Now, what is so important that you could not wait your turn?"

## CHAPTER 23

**VICTORIA RAMOS LED LORENZO** down a long hall and into a large room at the end. The hall was lined with bookshelves packed with what looked to him like law books—state statutes, court decisions, whatever reference work any attorney needed to practice.

Her office was spare but tasteful: an oak roll-top desk and swivel chair, two visitor chairs, a large table, some antique "stacker" bookcases, and a few oak filing cabinets. The wooden floor was covered with several brightly colored Navajo rugs.

"I love the way you've furnished your office," he said, as he sat in one of the chairs. "Very tasteful. Are these pieces all antiques?" It was time to discard his *peón* demeanor.

She raised an eyebrow and looked angry. "The people who usually sit where you are do not know a thing about antique furniture. Who are you, and why are you here taking my valuable time? Are you investigating me or selling something?"

Lorenzo pulled out his wallet and produced his Oregon lawyer credentials and a business card. She scanned them quickly and returned the credentials. She also seemed to relax a bit.

"It is good to meet you, Mr. Madrid."

"Please call me Lorenzo."

"Lorenzo it will be. And I'm Victoria. What can I do for you? You certainly don't want a job. And why are you dressed like you just sneaked across the border?"

"I need to explain," he said, a sheepish look on his face. "I figured I wouldn't be as conspicuous dressed like this as I would in a three-piece pinstripe with matching tie and handkerchief."

"That I agree with."

"I know you're busy, but I wanted to drop by to explain why I need your help."

Her eyebrow went up again. "My help to do what?"

"I'm teaching a course in immigration law this semester at the UCLA School of Law. I want to give the students a taste of the world you deal with every day. I do the same thing in my practice in Salem, Oregon—or at least I did."

"Oh, so you've closed your practice?"

He paused and decided this was not the time or the place to talk about himself. And certainly not to a stranger. A beautiful stranger, but still a stranger.

"Yeah. Long story, but too boring to go into now." Lorenzo leaned forward. "My plan is to bring four of my students over here for a few days to gather information about the practice of law in East L.A. I hoped they might be able to talk with you and maybe observe how you work with your clients. They could also do research for you. And maybe you could suggest other people they might talk to around here."

She was quiet for so long that Lorenzo thought she was going to turn him down.

"I should talk this over with my co-worker here at the clinic, Ronaldo Soto." She thought for a moment, then said, "But I run this place, and I want to do this. We'll all benefit from it—the students, me, maybe my clients. It's a very interesting idea."

She paused and looked at Lorenzo. "Would you be here with them?"

"I could be, sure," he said. "I only teach two days a week."

"You know I don't have a lot of time. My schedule is packed from morning till night, so I have no time to hold the hands of a bunch of college students."

"There would only be four of them," he said. "They'll gather the material and prepare lectures for the rest of the class."

"Good," she said. "I could let you use a small office for the days you are here."

Lorenzo was smiling. "That sounds ideal," he said, standing up and offering his hand. "Another thing just occurred to me. I know this neighborhood. In fact, I grew up here."

"You did?" She looked surprised. The eyebrow went up again.

"Another long, boring story. Anyway, I know that this has never been a safe area, especially for strangers. I'm concerned about my students."

Victoria Ramos shook her head, stood up, and walked to the door. "Oscar," she called to someone down the hall. "Please come to my office."

Lorenzo blinked at the sight of a man whose massive body filled the doorway. He must have weighed at least three hundred pounds. He was well over six feet tall, had a shaved head, and sported the tattoos of a gang member. The scowl on his face changed to a smile as he looked at Victoria.

"This is Oscar, my bodyguard."

Lorenzo tried not to wince when the huge man shook his hand. He hoped no bones had been broken.

"If he can keep me safe, he can certainly watch over a bunch of wet-behind-the-ears college students!"

## CHAPTER 24

**BY THIS TIME,** the wound on Perez's face had quit bleeding. Although it throbbed a bit, it had not been deep enough to do permanent harm. He was seething inside but had to appear calm until he figured out how to deal with this dangerous lunatic.

"Hugo wasn't very smart," he said to Pantera, who was sitting at the table again, drinking shot glass after shot glass of tequila. After each one, he would snap his fingers to have his hapless assistant, Felix, fill it again.

"That is obvious. Why did you keep him around? You have to be a little bit smart . . ." He paused and held up a hand with the thumb and forefinger almost touching.

The other men began to sneer and laugh at Perez.

*"Silencio!"* shouted Pantera. "I will tell you when to talk and when to laugh and who to laugh at! Right, Felix?"

*"Sí, señor."*

"I believe a question is hanging in the air, Perez. Why did you hire Hugo?"

"I didn't hire him," replied Perez. "He was sent by someone down here to help me in Oregon. I could tell right away that he didn't have much up here." He pointed to his head. "But I had no one else."

"Okay, okay, I get it," said Pantera, wiping his mouth after taking another drink.

This man is a drinker, thought Perez. That makes him vulnerable. And he may be going blind. He even squinted at the glass and lifted the tequila bottle close to his face, as if he's having trouble reading the label. Probably has syphilis of the brain from years of whoring.

"Let us get back to the subject at hand, this bastard Madrid. How do we find him and deal with him? I won't be satisfied until he's lying dead at my feet." Pantera's eyes were fixed on Perez as he waited for an answer.

"I watched outside the building where he lived in Oregon and saw the police standing around and the medical people remove the body Hugo thought was Madrid. I asked some neighbors what had happened. No one knew anything except for an old woman who lived in the building too."

"Yes, yes! What did she tell you?"

"She knew Madrid mostly by sight and said he was a nice man. Then she whispered that she thought he was, as she called it, a fairy."

Pantera looked perplexed. "He worked magic somehow? He was a magician who waved . . . what do you call it?" He turned to Felix.

"A wand, *señor*."

"Yes, yes, a wand, of course."

"No, *señor*," said Perez, barely able to hide a smirk. "That is what some older people in America call someone who is gay... homosexual."

"*MARICÓN!*" shouted Pantera. "That is very interesting. So maybe he was balling the kid Hugo killed? That gives us something to go on. Maybe Hugo saw Madrid go into that place and figured it was where he lived. But the kid lived there." He thought for a moment. "So maybe Hugo did not deserve to die." More contemplation. "But he was still a dumb ass. We don't need any more dumb ass guys around here."

He waved his arm toward the others and turned to Perez. "Not including you, of course," he said with a smirk. "I know one thing for sure. We've got to find this cocksucker Madrid. If he's here, we've got to find him and kill him."

"It's a big city, *señor*," said Felix, daring to speak without being spoken to.

Pantera turned to him and motioned him closer. He grabbed him by the shoulders and pulled him close, then grabbed his testicles and squeezed them hard. Felix screamed and fell backwards.

"You're a good assistant, my little *amigo*," he snarled. "But you will speak when I tell you to speak. Agreed?"

Felix nodded as he struggled to his feet and sat down in a chair farther down the table.

Pantera turned back to Perez.

"It **is** a big city," said Perez.

"So are jungles," responded Pantera, "where a panther always gets his prey."

## ESTEBAN PEREZ'S STORY

*As children in Mexico, Esteban and his sister, Margarita, were very close. They lived with their parents in a middle-class section of Guadalajara and went to an expensive private school. Their father worked on the railroad as a maintenance superintendant. Because of that job, he was gone for weeks at a time, inspecting locomotives, train cars, and roadbeds all over the country.*

*Their mother stayed at home with them, although a full-time nurse took care of them much of the time because she was gone a lot too. Because her husband made a good income, their mother fancied herself as being part of a higher social class than she really was. In her mind, she was a socialite, attending luncheons and dinners and doing charity work for the poor. Her lack of style and sophistication made her the butt of jokes—all behind her back, of course—by the society women she was trying to emulate.*

*The children did well in school. Both were smart and got good grades, when they studied. Margarita was a favorite of several of the nuns who showered her with attention and forgave her late assignments and occasional tantrums.*

*Esteban did not fare as well with the priests who were his teachers. He was forever getting into schoolyard fights. When that happened, he was whacked on the behind, often as much as twenty-five times. He refused to cry or beg for the priest to stop hitting him, which would often make the priest angry and he would hit him even more. One day after school, the monsignor who was in charge caught him having sex in a closet with another student, a fourteen-year-old girl. Because her father was an important man in town, the school authorities expelled Esteban permanently. With no school to attend, his father out of town, and his mother attending some luncheon or dinner or other event, Esteban spent a lot of time roaming around town. There he got to know kids his own age who had never been to school and who knew how to have a good time. He also met members of the various street gangs in town.*

*Margarita's downfall came after their father was killed in a railroad accident. She had always been his favorite child, and he spoiled her and paid more attention to her than Esteban. She was distraught and spent days and days in her room crying. When she went to school, she couldn't concentrate. She began to neglect her homework and, before long, she was not going to school at all.*

*While their mother was away, visiting her sister as a way to ease her own grief, Margarita invited a different boy into her bed each night. Although only sixteen, she looked older, with beautiful black hair, dark eyes, and the figure of a mature woman. Soon the boys in her bed were replaced by men—horny and often old and ugly, but always rich men.*

*"All they need is a lot of money to pay me and the equipment to do the job," she said to her brother. Preoccupied with his own descent into depravity, Esteban only listened. Her life is her life, just like my life is my life, he thought.*

*Several years passed and not much changed in the Perez household. Their mother became more grandiose in her attitude, especially after she received a large insurance settlement and a permanent income from the railroad. She* started bringing home rich men to share her bed.

Margarita was still doing the same.

One night Esteban confronted her. "Margarita, why are you throwing away your life? You sleep with any man who comes along. You drink too much. Are you taking drugs? Most of the time you look terrible. You are a beautiful woman, but your looks are rapidly disappearing."

Margarita was sitting at a mirror, applying makeup.

"Do you think that heavy stuff on your face will hide the circles under your eyes and the blotches on your skin?"

"What business is it of yours, Esteban? You have become nothing more than a gangster. All this talk about Señor Robles. Señor Robles this and Señor Robles that. Are you his little toy? Does he take you to bed, is that what he does?"

Esteban walked behind her and put his hands on her throat. "How dare you say that about a man I respect!" He felt his hands tighten, and she soon began to gasp for breath. Then he shook his head in disbelief at what he was doing and released his grip.

Margarita began coughing and grabbed a long nail file from the table and stabbed it into his hand. "Get out, get out!" she screamed. "I never want to see you again! You are dead to me!"

He turned and ran from the room, holding his wounded hand.

Unwilling to go home after this incident, Esteban fell deeper into the world of street gangs and drug dealers. It was in this world that he had met Ernesto Robles, the ruthless boss of a large cartel. At the time he and Margarita had argued so violently, he was only a lowly member of the Robles organization.

# DANGER IN UNLIKELY PLACES

*Soon Robles noticed that Esteban was very smart, so he began to treat him like the son he never had. Esteban rose in the organization and was soon handling all of what Robles called "sensitive projects": collecting money, arranging meetings for Robles with the bosses of the other cartels, and directing men to deal with the enemies of the cartel. He was soon spending all of his time at the Robles hacienda.*

*Given the estrangement with his mother and the disgust he felt about what his sister had become, he abandoned both and never saw them again.*

*Three years later, Esteban was in charge of the southern part of the Robles territory in Mexico. There, he thrived and was soon one of Robles's top lieutenants.*

*When Robles was killed at his ranch in Oregon, Esteban took it hard. He wished he had been the one to die.*

*A few days later, Esteban stood beside the coffin and gazed at Robles's body. "Whoever did this to you will pay dearly," he muttered. "I will hunt him down and kill him."*

*He vowed to seek revenge on the person who killed the only father he ever cared about. He would avenge the death of his beloved* Señor *Robles.*

*A name soon surfaced, handed to him on a slip of paper by one of the men who had been in Oregon.*

*The name was* **Lorenzo Madrid.**

# CHAPTER 25

LORENZO SMILED TO HIMSELF as he drove out of Boyle Heights and into the downtown area of Los Angeles. Things had gone well at the clinic, and he was pleased that his students would be getting a first-hand look at one of the consequences of illegal immigration.

As a kid growing up, he had often looked at the tall buildings of the central city. Then, they had looked like magical towers where well-dressed people went in and out every day to do important things. As a little brown kid, he could only dream that he would ever be a part of that life. Now, with luck and help, he was at that point.

His mind on the past and his future, Lorenzo did not at first see that a low-riding Chevrolet with tinted windows had begun to follow him. The street was lined with stores selling everything from groceries and liquor to the services of a palm reader. And the proprietors of each one had their radios tuned to a different Mexican station. The cacophony of the different sounds was deafening.

At a stop light, the car pulled up next to him, its driver gunning the engine as if challenging him to a race. When the light changed, Lorenzo ignored him and drove away slowly so he could fall behind.

At the next signal, the same thing happened, although this time Lorenzo got a good look at the driver. A man about thirty with the unmistakable tattoos of a gang member on his neck and arms was smiling at him and giving him the finger.

"Hey, *el jefe*. You lost or somethin'? You better get the fuck outta here," he shouted, then turned to laugh with his passenger.

Lorenzo gunned the engine as the light changed, although he had little faith that this old car would outpace the Chevy. He went through the next light even after it had changed to red, followed by the Chevy. The tires squealed as he turned a number of corners onto streets where he had learned to drive. He managed to keep just out of reach; however, the Chevy was right behind him and the driver was attempting to bump him and push him off the street and into the curb or a tree.

At one point, Lorenzo saw a railroad track ahead with a train bearing down on the crossing. The warning gate had already started to go down as Lorenzo stepped on the gas. He thought he could make it through the opening, but then he heard a bang. When he looked back, he saw that the rear window was smashed into hundreds of pieces. The car could still move and, as he drove away, he glanced back at the other car between the spaces of the moving train cars. In what looked like the jerky motion of a silent movie, the goons were running around their car, waving guns, in a dance of defeat.

Lorenzo pulled over in front of an abandoned house, grabbed the car rental papers and the keys, got out and ran down the street. He ducked into the alcove of another abandoned building and pulled out his cell phone. He punched in a number and waited for the call to go through.

"This is Greg Nettles, of the Drug Enforcement Administration office in Portland, Oregon," said the recorded message. "Leave your name and number, and I will get back to you as soon as I can. Please be aware that, although this is a secure line, the call may be monitored for security purposes."

"Greg. It's Lorenzo. We need to talk. Please call me back—fast!"

## CHAPTER 26

**PEREZ WAS WATCHING PANTERA FIGHT TO STAY AWAKE** as he nodded off. Some super *el jefe,* he thought, smiling to himself. This man is vulnerable. I can take out this man.

Pantera was roused from his nap by one of his bodyguards who knelt down and whispered into his ear.

"I told you never to disturb my sleep!" He yawned. "Who did you say is here?"

More whispering. Pantera turned to Perez. "You know two *hombres* called Nestor and Saul?"

"Yeah, they are my guys. They keep an eye out for me in Boyle Heights."

"Where is that?"

"East of downtown. Not far from here."

"Bring their sorry asses in here," Pantera said to his man.

The two men came in and walked toward the table. They were stopped by Pantera's other bodyguard. He patted them down.

They nodded at Perez. *"Buenos días, Señor* Perez."

He nodded at them. "What do you? . . ."

"Shut up, Perez!" said Pantera. "I am in charge here." He turned to the men. "What do you have to report to your *jefe?*"

They looked confused and their heads turned from Pantera to Perez.

"It is okay to talk," Perez told them. "This is *Señor* Pantera, who has come from Mexico to check on us."

Pantera got up and faced the men, his feet apart and arms at his side, as if he was a general standing at attention to review his troops. He squinted at them and snapped his fingers. He stooped to allow Felix to put eyeglasses on him.

"Speak!"

The men squared their shoulders and talked. "We were cruising around the neighborhood and hanging around the legal clinic like you told us to . . ." Nestor glanced at Perez, "when we saw a tall man walk in and go up to the main desk."

"Yes, yes," said Pantera, impatiently.

"My sister-in-law Gloriana works there for the *Señorita* Victoria Ramos. I got her to step outside so I could find out who this guy was."

"Yes, yes!" More impatience from Pantera.

Perez nodded for Nestor to go on with his story.

"Gloriana said he did not have an appointment, and he seemed mad when she would not let him go inside to see the *señorita*. Just then, *Señorita* Ramos came out and led him back to her office."

"What did this man look like?" asked Perez. "Like the guy in the photo I gave you?"

"Photo?" said Pantera. "Why do I not know about this photo?"

I'll show this fucker who takes care of business, thought Perez. "On a hunch, when I heard that Madrid might be coming to L.A., I circulated his photo to my men in case they saw him. I got it off the Internet." He turned to Nestor and Saul. "Was it him?"

"I think so, but we could not tell for sure," answered Nestor.

"Was he good looking, like a movie star? That's what people say about him. How was he dressed? In a suit and tie, like a lawyer?"

"No, *Señor* Perez," Saul replied. "From what we could tell, he looked like one of us—I mean, he wore jeans and a work shirt and a straw hat."

Pantera was being surprisingly quiet during this interrogation.

"We followed him when he left that place," Saul continued.

"So, where did he go?" asked Perez.

"I think he made us when we pulled up next to him," said Saul. "He started driving real fast and zigged and zagged and beat us to a train crossing where we lost him."

"Lost him?" screamed Pantera.

Nestor and Saul looked at Perez, who gave them a nod of reassurance.

"Here I thought we had something," moaned Pantera as he sat down, his hands covering his head. "Must I do everything?"

He glanced at Felix, who filled his glass with another shot of tequila.

## CHAPTER 27

**LORENZO'S CELL PHONE WAS RINGING** as he unlocked the door of his house two hours later. He had taken a bus to Union Station, where he changed to a cab for the drive to Westwood. During the whole trip, he had checked to make sure he was not being followed.

"Greg, thanks for getting back to me so fast."

"You still in L.A.?"

"Yep, I'm still here."

"So, what's the hurry? Are you okay?"

"So far, but that might be changing."

Lorenzo quickly filled his friend in on his visit to the legal clinic and the encounter with the two gang members.

"Not good, not good," said Greg. "You know you should get out of L.A. right now. Maybe even go into Witness Protection."

"You and I know that I can't do that, Greg. I'm committed to my job here, and it looks like it might lead to something I'd like to do, I mean as a career."

"I knew you'd say that."

There was silence on the line.

Lorenzo walked into the living room and sat down as he waited.

"Okay," said Greg finally. "Here's what we're going to do for now. I have a friend on the LAPD Narcotics Task Force, Jane Berman. She's actually in charge of it. She used to be one of us, I mean, she was in the DEA. I worked with her in Florida. She's tough and very good at what she does. I'm going to call her and tell her all about you to see if she can help us."

"Us?" asked Lorenzo. "I appreciate your help, of course, but you're in Oregon, and I'm down here."

"Yeah, but Lorenzo, you helped us break up the Robles cartel. We owe you something for that, especially if this situation is a direct result of your work for us."

"I guess I do need your help, Greg. This is beginning to worry me."

"Sit tight for now. Go about your business but be careful. What will you be doing later today?"

"I don't have a class, but I have to go to another reception at the dean's house tonight at six."

"Keep your phone with you, and I'll be in touch."

## CHAPTER 28

**THE DEAN HELD THESE FACULTY RECEPTIONS** at his home once a month. Lorenzo had always hated such useless social gatherings, but according to his colleagues in the law school, they were command performances. So he showered and changed out of his peasant outfit from East L.A., into a dress shirt, gray slacks, and a blazer.

As he had before, his student Asa Long opened the door.

"Hello again, Professor Madrid. Come in. The other professors are outside in the garden. I guess you remember the way."

"I do. By the way, I've spent part of today in Boyle Heights arranging for our research over there. I'll tell you all about it in class tomorrow."

"Fantastic! Can't wait."

The doorbell rang again, and Long hurried to open the door. Lorenzo started to walk down the hall to the garden when a bejeweled arm grabbed him and pulled him into a large room that was filled with works of art.

"Lorenzo," said Margarita, the dean's wife. "I need to get to know you better." She locked her arm into his and, for a moment, he couldn't shake it off.

He gulped. "Mrs. Askew. Nice to see you again."

"Margarita. Please call me that, *señor*."

He cleared his throat nervously. "Where is your husband?"

"Oh, he's running around someplace," she said in a dismissive way. "We live separate lives. He has the law and the school, and I have . . ." she looked around, "my freedom to do as I wish." She dug her fingers into his arm. "Look, I will not beat around the bush—that is not my style. You are a very attractive man, a very attractive Latin man. I want to get to know you better, in every sense of that word."

Lorenzo knew he didn't want her kind of trouble. Was this the time to play the gay card—to tell her he did not swing in her direction?

"Mrs. Askew and Professor Madrid."

Both of them turned to see Leslie Mason standing in the doorway. "May I join you?"

"Absolutely," said Lorenzo, relieved to be rescued from the clutches of the dean's wife.

"Miss . . . Mason is it?" said Margarita, looking more than a bit annoyed. "I was just showing Professor Madrid our collection of Mexican art."

"And your etchings?" Mason smiled sweetly.

The sarcasm was lost on the dean's wife. "Etchings? I know nothing of art, but I believe my husband said these were oil paintings."

Both Lorenzo and Leslie hid their smiles and began to walk around the room, murmuring comments about the quality of the paintings as they passed each one.

"There you are, my darling," said the dean, as he walked into the room. "I wondered where you had gone."

"I was just taking care of our guests," said Margarita. "Someone has to do that."

"Ah, Professors Mason and Madrid. Good to see you again, Lorenzo. Settling in okay? I've been on a fundraising trip. Seems like all I do is hit the road to raise money. Right, my darling?"

Margarita embraced her husband tightly. As she did so, she stared at Lorenzo, licked her lips, and winked.

"Let's go join the others," said the dean. "I've heard rumors that food and drink can be found somewhere around here."

As the four of them walked out the doors to the garden, Lorenzo whispered to Leslie, "Thanks for rescuing me."

The gathering was smaller this time than the one the month before. Lorenzo spotted Etta Mae Bishop dancing with Vladimir Volga, and George Haller was standing near the bar with a martini glass in his hand. He nodded at the other faculty members as Leslie led him to a table on the far side of the patio. A waiter was standing nearby to take their orders.

"Gin and tonic," said Leslie.

"Dos Equis," said Lorenzo. Then to Leslie, "Is the dean's wife always that forward?"

"From what I've heard. When I saw you in there with her, I realized you might need to be rescued. Everyone knows about her except the dean. She is not very discrete in what she does. That might be fine in Mexico, but it doesn't go over well in the United States."

"Yeah, we are pretty prudish when it comes to sex," he said. "In many other Western countries, husbands have girlfriends and wives have lovers and no one cares—and they all know one another."

They quit talking when the waiter arrived with their drinks.

"Is this an exclusive non-White club or can anyone join?"

Etta Mae Bishop pulled up a chair and sat down; Vladimir Volga sat next to her.

"Nice to be seeing you again," said Volga, in his usual fractured English. "I think our busyness has kept us apart this semester."

"Don't you love the way he speaks English?" said Etta Mae. "I love that about you, my little babushka."

"A babushka is an old woman or a shawl," said Volga. "I am not either one of those, the last time I have looked at myself."

They all laughed. After a half-hour of eating and drinking, the dean tapped a fork on his glass.

"Margarita and I are so glad to have you in our home," he said to everyone. "You represent the future of this law school. Any college thrives on the quality of its faculty . . . and the quality of its students. We have several of them here with us tonight. Please step out and be recognized."

Hesitatingly, Asa Long and three other students, who Lorenzo did not know, stopped serving drinks and food and stepped forward. The guests applauded, and the four students took bows before returning to their work.

Soon, George Haller walked over to them, a bit unsteady on his feet. His eyes were bloodshot, and he had food crumbs in his bushy mustache.

Lorenzo got up to guide him to a chair. "Kind of a tight squeeze," he said, as he pulled out a chair and helped Haller sit down.

"So, how are all of you newbies doin'?" Haller's speech was slurred. "Did you get a load of the dean's whore parading around like she owns the place."

"I guess she does," said Etta Mae. "She **is** married to the dean."

Haller glared at her. "That was a figure of speech, my dear. Or don't you people know what that is."

"My people!" thundered Etta Mae in a voice that probably could be heard on campus. "Do you think of me as some kind of African refugee?"

"Put up your fists!" yelled Volga. "I do not like it that you spoke that way to my dear friend Etta Mae."

Lorenzo and Leslie exchanged glances and stood up.

"Come on, Etta," said Leslie. "Let's take a walk out in the garden. It should be very nice at this time of day."

As they walked away, Lorenzo nudged Volga back into his chair and raised his hand to signal a waiter. "How about some coffee?"

In the meantime, Haller had fallen asleep and was totally oblivious to the commotion his words had caused.

As soon as he could do so gracefully, Lorenzo headed for the door.

"Professor Madrid, someone is waiting to see you," Asa said, as Lorenzo stepped outside.

A middle-aged woman was standing next to a plain sedan parked in the driveway. She stepped forward with what looked like official credentials in one hand.

"Jane Berman, LAPD. I used to work with Greg Nettles, and he asked me to look you up. Is there somewhere we can talk in private?"

## CHAPTER 29

**THE MORE ESTEBAN PEREZ WAS AROUND PANTERA,** the more he hated him. He was little more than a two-bit gangbanger who wasn't very smart. He was extremely ruthless, and Perez suspected that he had gotten where he was in the organization by killing all his rivals—or by having them killed. He also used his height well, towering over most everyone else. And then there were his tattoos, especially the one on his face. If given a choice, even Perez would have avoided someone who looked like him had they met in a dark alley.

That still did not explain why Pantera was where he was. Perez could not understand why the men who controlled the cartel in Mexico had put this common cutthroat—this *asesino*—in charge of the west coast operations in America. Especially when Perez was more qualified.

Pantera appeared to be dozing, so no one said a word, lest a noise send him into one of his rages. Nestor and Saul were still standing in front of him, casting nervous glances at Perez from time to time.

As they waited for Pantera to wake up, Perez thought about his situation. No question about it, this man was a psychopath and not fit to run the organization. Perez vowed to do all he could to get rid of him. As witness to that vow, he crossed himself and fingered the small cross he wore on a chain around his neck. His mother had given it to him years ago, and he had never taken it off. More than once, it had helped him endure hard times and tight situations.

"Are you some kind of religious nut?" asked Pantera, suddenly opening his eyes, as if he sensed Perez's intentions.

"My mother gave it to me," said Perez through gritted teeth. "I was praying for your success as our leader."

What bullshit, thought Perez, but if this idiot was nothing else, he was vain and susceptible to flattery. The ploy appeared to work.

"Goddamn fucking right," Pantera said. "But with my skills, we don't need any prayers. Right, Felix?"

"*Sí, señor*," said his assistant, his voice shaking.

The others joined in as if in a chorus. "*Sí, señor.*"

Pantera turned to Nestor and Saul. "So, was it him or not?" He obviously forgot that they had already answered that question.

The two glanced nervously at Perez, who nodded slightly.

"We think so."

"Think so!" Pantera shouted. "You either saw him or you didn't!"

They looked at each other. "It was him," they said in unison.

"What was he doing there, I wonder?" said Perez. "He is a lawyer in Oregon, so he would not need legal help at a free clinic."

"Places like that are for wetbacks, like you guys," said Pantera disdainfully. "I myself have only the best attorneys in Mexico at my disposal—the very best attorneys in all of Mexico."

Then Perez asked them again about how Madrid had been dressed and what kind of car he had been driving. "He went there for a reason that had little, if anything, to do with the law," said Perez, daring to speak without Pantera's permission. "And, according to Nestor and Saul, he was wearing work clothes as a disguise."

"What is disguise?" asked Pantera.

*"Disfraz,"* said Perez. "He was hiding his true identity to blend into the neighborhood over there. You do not wear a three-piece suit and a tie in Boyle Heights."

A look of embarrassment crossed Pantera's face but only for a moment. "I knew that," he said with a wave of his hand.

Perez turned to Nestor and Saul. "I want the two of you to go back to the clinic and wait for Madrid to return. He's bound to come back, and when he does, we will nab him." Then he looked at Pantera. "With your permission, of course, *mi jefe*."

## CHAPTER 30

**BECAUSE HE LIVED SO CLOSE** to the dean's house, Lorenzo invited Jane Berman to go there with him.

"Wow, this is definitely how the other half lives," she said when she stepped inside.

He led her into the living room, and they sat down facing each other in chairs on either side of the fireplace.

"My reaction too, every time I walk into this place," he said. "It's not mine. The law school provides it for visiting faculty. It's way beyond anything I can afford. But I love it. Can I get you something to drink? Coffee, tea, water?"

"No, but thanks. I can't stay long. I'm about to go on shift. I am unlucky enough to be working graveyard tonight." She paused and looked directly at Lorenzo. "Greg said you think some gang members are after you. He filled me in on your run-in with the Robles organization. Tell me why you think they're after you now."

Lorenzo told Berman about the car that followed him from the clinic and his successful escape.

"They could have just been cruising the neighborhood. Those guys love to parade around in their souped-up cars. They don't do much all day except hang out and try to look mean."

"Since Greg told me about what happened to Chad Dunbar in Oregon, I've been paying attention to my surroundings. I was extra paranoid when I drove over to Boyle Heights, because I was afraid that anyone looking for me might go there. I mean, Hispanic guys are known to gravitate toward their own people."

"And I guess the bad guys thought the same thing," Berman said.

Lorenzo shrugged. "Unfortunately. The irony is that I wouldn't go near that area under normal circumstances."

Berman had a quizzical look on her face. "And why is that?"

"I left that world behind a long time ago. I grew up over there, and I don't want anything to do with it now. I have devoted a lot of my career to helping **my** people, but I came down here to do something else."

"So why'd you drive over there in the first place?"

Lorenzo told her about the legal clinic and his plan to take his interns there to learn about practicing immigration law firsthand.

"Given your situation with the gangs and all, do you think that's still a smart idea?" asked Berman. "These guys don't give up. If you're marked, you're marked. And you also might be putting your students in danger."

Lorenzo thought for a moment before answering. "I came down here to do a job, and I'm not going to let a bunch of two-bit hoods keep me from that goal," he said, eyes flashing.

Berman frowned. "Okay, I take your point. But . . ."

"Besides, they've got a security guard working there every day, and I don't plan on any night work."

Berman shook her head, a chagrined look on her face. Then she stood up. "Here's my card. I've written my cell number on the back. Call me if you see anyone or anything suspicious. Will you do that?"

"I promise," he said, shaking her hand. "Thank you for dropping by. It was good to meet you."

"Greg says you're a good person and that you really helped him out," she said. "I'm still a DEA agent in my heart, I guess. Just couldn't take the constant stress. But I can still speak for all my former pals, including Greg—I think we owe you for that one."

# CHAPTER 31

**AFTER CLASS THE NEXT DAY,** Lorenzo drove the four interns to East L.A. for their first visit to the legal clinic. He had ordered an unmarked university van. They left the opulence of West L.A. and drove through the high-rise buildings of downtown and then to the decaying neighborhoods of East L.A. There they saw a mix of well-kept bungalows and abandoned buildings.

Their comments were revealing. Only Nathan was shocked by what he saw.

"I have only seen true poverty in China," he said. "This is nothing like that. I mean, it does not look that bad on the surface. Some of these houses are nice and others look awful, like I imagine drug houses would look."

"Have you ever seen a drug house?" asked Cecilia.

He shook his head. "Only in the movies."

"Well, the reality is quite a bit different," she said, shaking her head. Lorenzo drove on but kept quiet and listened to the fascinating conversation.

"You ain't seen nothin' until you've seen a drug house that serves Black people," said Alex. "Only the baddest of the bad go to those places."

Asa was the only student to remain quiet, seeming to Lorenzo to be content to listen. His childhood might have been better than the others, although Lorenzo doubted that. He decided that now was not the time to intrude. They drove in silence for a while, watching the passing parade of people—a mix of parents with little kids, old people, and thugs—with only an occasional police car driving by.

"We're here. Let me take you inside to meet Victoria and her staff."

### ASA LONE EAGLE'S STORY

*My mom overdosed on crack cocaine when I was seven. The problem was that I was the only one with her at the time. It was winter on the rez and very cold. It was in North Dakota, you see. Pine Ridge.*

*She was always sweet to me, even when she was high, but when I was home, I always tried to stop her from taking drugs. One night, I was studying in the kitchen, and I heard a sound in the other room I had learned to dread: like uncorking a bottle. I knew she was filling a syringe with dope.*

*As I ran into the room, she ran out the front door. It had been snowing and was bitterly cold. I tried to tackle her so I could drag her back inside, but she was too fast for me and kept running. Then she stumbled and fell into a snow bank.*

*I reached her and tried to pull her up, but she was too strong and I was too little. All I could do was lie there with her head in my hands and watch her die. No one found us for a long time, and I had bad frostbite on both hands. I went to live with my granny after that.*

## CHAPTER 32

**PEREZ'S CELL PHONE RANG THE NEXT AFTERNOON** while he was moving to a small room at the rear of the building. Asshole that he was, Pantera had taken over the larger room Perez had been using for his office.

"As the true leader," he had said, "I am entitled to the bigger room."

"Whatever you want, *el jefe*. You are the boss!" Perez almost choked on the words, but knew he had to say them.

For now, Pantera had put himself in charge, and he had the men to back him up.

"Speak to me!" Perez yelled into the phone. He had learned long ago to use anger and abruptness as a tactic to keep his men in line. He paid them well, both in cash and drugs, so he didn't have to be nice to them too.

It was one of his men from Boyle Heights.

"Which one are you? Nestor or Saul?"

"Nestor, *Señor* Perez."

"Yes, Nestor. What do you have to report to me?"

"Saul and me, we've been waiting down the street from that legal place in East L.A."

"*Sí, sí.* And?"

"And we waited for a long time and got coffee and some good *tamales* at a small bodega over there."

"Great fuckin' *tamales, patrón!*" Perez could hear Saul yelling in the back.

"He's right, *patrón*. They're really good."

"I don't need to know what you ate or where you ate it," hissed Perez. "What the fuck did you see? Did Madrid come to the clinic like before?"

"*Sí, señor.* About an hour ago. He was driving a big van with state license plates on it. Some kids got out—three men and a woman—and went inside."

"And? What happened next?"

"I don't know. We couldn't go inside, and the windows were covered with curtains so we couldn't see anything."

"And what about this van he was driving. Was it official?"

"Official, *señor?*"

"Like from a government agency or a school?" Perez was starting to lose his patience.

"Well..."

"Well, what?"

"There was no writing on the doors, if that's what you mean."

"But it did not look like Madrid's vehicle?"

"Vehicle, *señor?*"

Perez let out a sigh of exasperation. "Like a car or a truck?"

"Not a car or a truck," said Nestor, trying to help. "A van."

Perez gritted his teeth but did not lash out at Nestor, a tactic that would not work with him.

"There was something else," Nestor said, pausing to think as if he had just recalled something important.

"Yes, yes!" shouted Perez.

"Saul walked by the van, you know kind of casual, and looked in at the driver's seat."

"And what did he see there, Nestor?"

"Some paperwork and it had some writing on it. What do the letters U C L and A stand for, *mi patrón?*"

## CHAPTER 33

**UNLIKE THE FIRST TIME LORENZO HAD COME TO THE CLINIC,** he and the students were ushered into Victoria Ramos's office right away. The receptionist's previous hostility had been replaced with extreme helpfulness.

"Nice to see you again, *señor*. May I get any of you a soft drink?"

Victoria got up from her desk and walked toward them as soon as they reached the doorway, arms extended. "Professor Madrid. Come in, please. And these are your students?" She turned to the four students and shook their hands enthusiastically.

While Lorenzo introduced each of them, he noticed a younger man standing awkwardly in the corner of the room. He walked over to him and extended his hand.

"Lorenzo Madrid. You must be Ronaldo Soto, Victoria's partner."

"Yes, I am. It is nice to meet you."

Victoria turned toward the two of them. "Where are my manners? This is my partner, Ronaldo Soto. You will be doing some of your work with him."

The other four walked over and shook his hand.

"Let's move across the hall to the conference room," said Victoria. "We'll have more room over there."

After they were seated, Victoria gave a presentation about the history of the legal clinic and its present goals.

"We are small, but we like to think we are mighty too," she said in closing. "And the reason is that we have the power of the law behind everything we do. In a free democracy like the United States, there is no power that is more important.

"These days, however, I'm afraid that the laws do not always work to the benefit of the thousands of law-abiding people who only want a better life here in this country. Now we have politics playing a very big role in determining immigration policy."

She paused and then asked, "Are any of you Republicans?"

Lorenzo and the four students shook their heads.

"Good. I shouldn't make this political, but facts are facts. Conservative members of Congress have been doing all they can to block the president's policies for a number of years, partly because they don't like him. But let's face it, another reason is that they don't want more brown people coming into this country. It's unfair and unjust, but it's true. They talk about terrorists slipping over the border. They rail against all the jobs the immigrants take away from the people they call 'real' Americans. That is all nonsense!"

Lorenzo noticed that all four students were nodding their heads in agreement. Of course, each one was part of a minority, including himself. He hadn't planned it that way, but it just worked out. He hoped that fact might make them more dedicated to the law in the future.

"After Republican members of Congress refused to overhaul the immigration system, the president came up with one of his own. His plan would block the deportation of undocumented children who arrived in this country before they were sixteen years old. He later added their parents to his protection plan. But twenty-six states filed suit to stop all of this and a conservative federal judge in Texas agreed with them and halted all programs."

Nathan raised his hand.

"Yes, Nathan."

"How does that affect your work here?"

Victoria sighed. "It makes it a lot harder. We deal more with people who are a bit older than the teenagers I mentioned before, but whole families are usually involved. A ruling like this puts the whole process in limbo. It is much harder to aid the often desperate people who come in here for help. Rules change so fast that we can't always keep up. But we have to try."

She looked around the table at each of them.

"And I hope you'll try too, if you choose to go into this kind of law. It will break your heart, but you'll also be greatly rewarded now and again, when this tattered system actually works."

She finished by asking, "Any questions?"

As Lorenzo figured he would, Alex had a tough one.

"Your people and my people have been kept down for centuries—and still are today," he said. "Why has the law failed us so many times?"

The others glanced at each other, looking pained and embarrassed that Alex had begun the internship in such a confrontational way.

Lorenzo agreed with Alex but decided to let Victoria answer.

"That is why we are here . . . is it Alex?"

"Yes, ma'am. Alex Wood."

"In your work with us over the next few days, maybe we can pick away at that mountain of failure."

At that moment, the receptionist walked into the room and whispered something to Victoria. She turned to Soto.

"Will you go over our plans with our guests, Ron? I need to step out for a minute. Will you join me, professor?"

Oscar, Victoria's bodyguard, was waiting for them in the hall.

"So, Oscar, what is so urgent?" she said a bit haughtily.

"I saw some men hanging around. They were looking at *Señor* Madrid's van, and I ran them off. Then I caught them walking close to the building and trying to see inside. I told them to leave once again and threatened them a little."

"What did they do?"

"They were punks and I am bigger. They took off after I slapped them around a bit and pushed them back out onto the street and to their car."

"What kind of car were they driving?" asked Lorenzo.

"A real gangbanger car—an old Chevy low-rider," he said.

"Do you know these guys?" Victoria asked Lorenzo.

"Only indirectly," he said.

## ALEX WOOD'S STORY

*My story's not all that different from other African American kids. Bad mother, no father, just the same. But the difference is I didn't have a grandma to turn to. Luckily, I had an older brother, Jeb. He took good care of me and my sister Rose as best he could, making sure we got to school and had food to eat. But he had to work to support us and was gone a lot.*

*So it was up to me to tend to Baby Rose. And I did the best I could. I made sure she ate supper and did her homework. I think she was in third grade, and I was in middle school at that time.*

*I studied hard and got good grades in every subject. I wanted to succeed so I could pay my brother back for all he had done for me. I wanted to buy a house so we could live together.*

*Shee-it! That was not gonna happen. I shoulda' known that.*

*One night my brother came home really late and really sick. I helped him undress and get into his bed, which was in the living room. He let Rose and me use the bedroom.*

*He went to sleep right away, and I went back to sleep. About an hour later, I heard him coughing real loud. I went in the living room, and he was moaning and thrashing around. I went over to him and saw that blood was pouring out of his mouth. It was all over the bed. I cradled his head in my arms and his eyes opened so fast it scared me. "Alex!" he shouted. And then he closed his eyes and I heard a kind of gurgling sound—then he stopped breathing.*

## DANGER IN UNLIKELY PLACES

*Rose and I were put in the foster care system after that. Lucky for me, I got taken in by a nice Black couple who encouraged me all through school and paid for college.*

*Rose? She wasn't so lucky. Last I heard, she was turning tricks in San Diego. Lots of sailors there, you know. Lots of need for her kind of skills.*

## CHAPTER 34

**WHEN NESTOR AND SAUL GOT BACK** and explained what had happened at the legal clinic, Perez shook his head disapprovingly. He kept his voice low so that Pantera, sleeping off the vast amount of tequila he had been drinking since he got there, would not hear. These were Perez's men, and he would handle it.

"And you let this guy push you around like that?"

"*Si señor*. He was very big," said Nestor.

"Bigger than us, that's for sure," added Saul, shaking his head.

"Who the fuck are you talking about?" shouted Pantera, as he staggered into the room.

Drinking was really a problem for Pantera, thought Perez. It was getting in the way of his ability to run the organization.

Nestor and Saul looked nervously at Perez before answering. He nodded to them—a move Pantera saw, even in his impaired state. "Why look at him?" he shouted. "You need to look at me!"

He pounded his chest. "I am *el jefe* around here! Do you understand?"

The two glanced at each other, then nodded vigorously and replied, *"Sí, Señor* Pantera."

"So, what's this all about?" continued Pantera.

"We were telling *Señor* Perez that we think we saw Lorenzo Madrid at the same legal clinic where we saw him before. He was driving a big van that looked kind of official. He brought some kids with him to the clinic."

"They were sick?" asked Pantera, truly puzzled. "This Madrid is a doctor?"

Perez barely contained the smirk on his face. You dumb fuck, he thought to himself, it is not a medical clinic.

"No, *Señor* Pantera, it is a legal clinic," he said. "People—our people, really poor people—go there for help with their legal problems: deportation, trouble with the law, that kind of thing."

"Oh, *sí.* Why didn't you say so? Very strange to me. This country does some crazy shit." Pantera said and turned to the two men. "Go on with your story."

"They looked like students. Maybe in their twenties. They drove up and then went inside."

"And what did you do about that?" shouted Pantera.

"Nothing, *señor*. What could we do? They walked in and closed the door."

"Well . . . you could have gone in there and brought him out at gunpoint." Pantera smiled at the thought. "And then brought him here to me. I want to look him in the eye, so he knows who I am and what I represent. Then I will teach him a lesson he will never forget."

He glanced at Perez. "Show me this stupid photo everyone is talking about!" he commanded.

Nestor handed Pantera the picture of Madrid. Pantera's eyes opened wide and gleamed with a menace Perez hadn't seen before. Was this why everyone seemed to fear him—that he was some kind of demon? Pantera began to rave, almost foaming at the mouth. Was he crazy or just drunk?

"I want to destroy him for what he did to *Señor* Robles and to our whole operation," shouted Pantera. "But first I want to make him suffer!"

## CHAPTER 35

**VICTORIA PULLED LORENZO INTO HER OFFICE** and closed the door.

"Do you know those guys or not? I need to know. I can't put my office in any danger from gangs."

Lorenzo started to answer, but she put up her hand to stop him.

"We have had an agreement with the ones that control the turf here in Boyle Heights for several years. They promised to leave us alone and consider us neutral because of all the good we do—for free—with their relatives and friends." She nodded that it was okay for him to speak.

"I have gotten involved in a situation that I really don't understand," he said. "As a result, I think some bad guys are after me."

"Bad guys as in gang members like the ones hanging around here today?" she said, shaking her head.

"I'm afraid so," he said, eyes downcast.

"Why would they be after you?"

Lorenzo told her about the death of Robles and how some of Robles's men blamed him. He also filled her in on Chad Dunbar's murder being caused by someone targeting him.

"I came down here to start a new chapter in my life, and all of this followed me," he continued. "But I didn't want to lead whoever these guys are—and I swear I don't know—to you here at the clinic. I am very sorry. I think we'd better call it all off and get the hell out of here!"

Victoria Ramos sat for a moment without saying anything.

"Look, Lorenzo, I believe you, and I like what you're doing and what you've done in the past. Like me, you care about people—our people, especially—and want only to help them. Let's finish up today like normal and then see what happens."

"I appreciate that, Victoria," he said, "but I can't let you do that. You don't owe me a thing. I can't . . ."

"But I want you to owe me," she said, smiling.

Lorenzo felt his face turning red. "Well . . . I don't know how to answer that."

She smiled again. "We'll see about that later."

"What about security? Oscar is big and strong, but he can't handle a whole gang."

"Oscar used to be in one of the worst gangs around here, and he still keeps up with his 'homies,' as he calls them," she said. "I'll get him to speak to his boys."

Lorenzo looked relieved. "You're sure you want to do this?"

She nodded. "Very sure. Let's go join the others."

↟ ↟ ↟

The students spent much of the day listening to Victoria and Soto talk about the kinds of cases they typically handled.

After that, with permission from the clients, they each sat in when the two attorneys met with those clients to discuss their cases. Lorenzo worked on his future lectures in the small office Victoria had given him.

When the day was over, they drove the van back to campus without incident.

---

### NATHAN CHEN'S STORY

*I guess I'm the lucky one of our group. My parents are well educated and successful. My dad is a doctor and my mom is a high school teacher. They encouraged me to excel all through school and I did. I was getting scholarships as early as my junior year in high school. My grades were so good that I got a full ride at Stanford. It was a cinch to get accepted to any law school I wanted to attend. I applied here at UCLA and was accepted. More scholarship money came my way, even though my parents had the money to pay for everything. They pay for my apartment in Westwood and give me a new car every year. I am lucky.*

*I cannot match the sad stories of my classmates, with one exception.*

*While I was growing up, I worshiped my grandfather—my father's father. After my grandmother died, he lived with us. He used to tell me stories of his years in China and Taiwan.*

*He joined the government of Chiang Kai-shek after he was overthrown by the Communists in 1949. They all fled to Formosa, which is what Taiwan was called then.*

*He wound up in intelligence as the assistant to the head of that government's CIA. He often hinted about what secrets he knew but never mentioned anything specific.*

*One day, when I was in high school, he and I were alone in the house, and there was a knock at the door. My grandfather walked into the front hall and opened it. I heard a gasp and when I ran to see what had happened to him, he was lying on the floor, grabbing at his neck.*

*I knelt down to help him, but he was dead within seconds. I never saw anyone run away from the house. My father said that Communist agents had killed him with a poisoned dart. I guess he was carrying too many past secrets in his head.*

## CHAPTER 36

**LORENZO STAYED LATE IN HIS OFFICE THAT NIGHT,** reading and taking notes from reference books about case law and articles in legal journals about the latest developments in immigration law. Then he spent some time writing in a journal he had started to keep several years before. By writing down his innermost thoughts, he had created a refuge from a world that had been chaotic and, at times lately, stressful for him. Things seemed more manageable if he wrote about them.

He was so wrapped up in tonight's musings that the time got away from him. When he looked at his watch, he was surprised to see that it was nearly midnight. He made sure he had the night pass Miss Stein had given him, in case he met a security guard. Then he placed the journal in the only desk drawer he could lock and turned off the light.

He walked down the hall and out the main door without seeing anyone. The moon was out as he headed west down Dickson Court.

He passed Dickson Plaza, the sunken area in front of Perloff Hall, the location of the School of Architecture. When he was an undergraduate, it had housed the art department. His outdoor commencement ceremony had been held here, and his parents had attended, looking both nervous and proud. It was rare for them to venture out of Boyle Heights into what his father called "the world of the *gringos*."

Lorenzo remembered being proud of them that day for making the sacrifices it took to pay for his college education. Later, his high GPA would earn him a full scholarship to law school. His smile faded as he remembered that both of them were now dead—and that his own predilections had brought on the shame his father felt toward him and probably caused the stroke that eventually killed him.

Lorenzo shook his head at the memory and walked on past Haines Hall toward his favorite building on campus, the magnificent Royce Hall.

If memory served him, Royce Hall was one of the four original structures built in the mid-1920s when the college moved from a downtown location to what was now Westwood.

As he reached the east end of that building, he became aware that someone was following him, but he saw no one when he looked back. He walked a bit farther and the feeling returned.

Was it the gangbangers from East L.A., so determined to get to him that they followed him even here to a high-class part of town they would never venture into during the day? There were many Hispanic students, as well as those around campus working on the grounds crews, but none of them looked like members of a drug gang.

Given what had happened, Lorenzo was in no mood to take any chances. He walked quickly into the colonnaded gallery that extended across the front of the huge building. Its tiled floors echoed the sound of his shoes. He had made it halfway across in front of the massive doors when he stopped again. He looked back in time to see a dark figure duck behind a pillar.

Lorenzo was no coward, but he didn't relish a confrontation with a thug carrying a gun or a knife. If this guy was determined to kill him, Lorenzo had to do something to thwart that plan. He rushed over to a smaller door that led to a side hall. Luckily, it was open. He ran down the dimly lit corridor, remembering that he had had several classes in the rooms opening off the hall. Unfortunately, all of the doors were locked.

He tried a door on the other side of the hall and, miraculously, it was unlocked. He stepped into the concert hall, a beautiful room that had withstood several earthquakes. He recalled from an architecture course he had taken in this very room that the designers of the building had used this large space to accentuate the grandeur of the Italian Romanesque-styled building. The ceiling was a series of gold and red tiled panels, and there were elaborate columns on opposite sides of the second-level boxes, which looked as if royalty should be seated in them to view a performance on stage.

It was in one these boxes that he decided to hide, at least for a time. He climbed up a spiral staircase near the stage and soon was standing behind the velvet curtain at the rear of the box. From here, he hoped to see who was following him and then decide what to do.

## CHAPTER 37

"DID YOU HEAR WHAT I SAID?" Pantera was shouting at Nestor and Saul.

Perez could see that they were really afraid of Pantera. The two had always been respectful of Perez and deferred to him as their leader, but they did not quake in his presence. Perez decided that Pantera's height and his tattoos added to his ability to intimidate.

"Look at me! I want to destroy this Lorenzo Madrid!" Now Pantera was standing in front of them, but they continued to stare at the floor.

"LOOK AT ME!" he shouted. *"COMPRENDE?"*

*"Sí, señor,"* they said in unison.

"I want you to go back out there and track this Madrid like you would a wild pig or a wild animal." He thought for a moment and smiled. "Like a panther, a panther like me!"

Pantera turned around and walked over to the large chair he insisted on sitting in at all times.

He thinks of it as some kind of throne, Perez had thought more than once.

"Now, get the fuck out of here and bring that *maricón* to me! When I am finished with him, he won't be a high-and-mighty lawyer for his people anymore! He'll be licking my boots. I will have his balls for breakfast!"

Turning to Felix, he shouted, "Bring those two whores to me now!"

## CHAPTER 38

**AFTER TEN MINUTES,** Lorenzo decided the danger had passed, and he could quit hiding and resume his walk home. Standing in the concert hall with no sound but his own breathing, he was feeling more than a little ridiculous.

He descended the spiral staircase and stepped out into the hall. He saw an exit sign on a door near the rear and walked toward it. It opened onto a cement path at the rear of Royce Hall. From here, he could walk down the hill and away from central campus.

"Lorenzo. Over here."

It was woman's voice, coming from the front of the building. Curiosity overcame his earlier fear, and he walked toward the sound. He stopped in the shadow of the colonnade and looked in the direction of the reflecting pool at the end of the plaza. A hooded figure was standing there. As he got closer, he could see who it was.

Margarita Askew let her long cloak fall to the ground, revealing her naked body. "You know you want me as much as I want you," she said breathlessly.

Before the astonished Lorenzo could answer, a shot rang out and Margarita fell into the pool.

Lorenzo reached into the pool and grabbed her around the shoulders to pull her out. He carefully placed her on her back on the pavement and began to administer CPR.

Just then, the beams of several flashlights shined on him.

"THIS IS THE POLICE! STEP AWAY FROM THE FOUNTAIN AND PUT YOUR HANDS WHERE WE CAN SEE THEM!"

## CHAPTER 39

**THREE POLICEMEN ADVANCED ON LORENZO** with their guns drawn. He put his hands behind his head, as he had seen countless "perps" do in movies and television shows.

"Shall I cuff him?" asked one of the men, who sounded young.

"No, but you better check out that body," said an older, more mature-sounding voice. Then turning to Lorenzo, he said, "You may put your hands at your sides. Who are you, and what are you doing here this late? Who is this woman, and what happened to her?"

"I can explain some of it," Lorenzo said to the policeman, who seemed to be in charge and had walked up next to him.

"Be my guest."

"My name is Lorenzo Madrid, and I am teaching immigration law this semester at the law school. I worked late tonight in my office back there." He gestured in the direction of the law school.

"Yeah. Go on."

"I was walking to my house in Westwood."

"YOU can afford to live in Westwood?" exclaimed the third cop. "That's rich. You people clean those houses, but live in them? I don't think so!"

It was irritating to Lorenzo that no matter how much time had passed, people were still as ignorant as ever.

"Ease up, Vern," said the cop in charge. "I'm handling this."

He turned back to Lorenzo. "Go on."

"As I got in front of Royce Hall, I felt that someone was following me. I could hear footsteps behind me, but I didn't see anyone. I'm kind of jumpy these days, so I..."

"Now why, pray tell, is that?" said Vern, the obnoxious cop. "You runnin' from somethin'?"

For a brief moment, Lorenzo considered telling them about the drug gang and his fear that they were after him, but he discarded that idea because he figured that none of these men would understand the subtleties of his situation.

"I was robbed up in Oregon a short time before I moved down here," he lied. "That has made me pretty cautious."

"Wow. Oregon," said the first cop who sounded younger than the others. "It rains a lot there, I guess. My girlfriend and I would like to..."

"Andy," said the cop in charge, "I'm trying to conduct an investigation here!"

"Sorry, boss."

"So you hid out. Where?"

"I ran into Royce Hall and found the door of the auditorium unlocked, so I ducked in there," said Lorenzo.

"Did anyone follow you?"

"No, I guess not. When it seemed safe, I walked out a back door and heard a woman call my name. By the time I got here, she had fallen into the pool," said Lorenzo, simplifying the timeline a bit. He gestured toward the lifeless form of Mrs. Askew. "Shouldn't we put something over her, to show some respect?"

"Do you know her?" asked the cop in charge, ignoring Lorenzo's suggestion.

"Yes. She is—was—the wife of the dean of the law school."

"And then you pulled her out of the water," continued the cop in charge. "And why was that?"

Lorenzo squelched his anger before answering. "To see if she was still breathing. I gave her CPR, in case there was still a chance, but I'm afraid she's dead."

"Looked to us like you was kissin' her on the mouth," said Vern, "and lovin' every minute of it! What happened to her clothes? You take 'em off her?"

Lorenzo couldn't help himself. "You idiot! I was trying to save Mrs. Askew!"

Vern lunged at Lorenzo, but the cop in charge held him back.

"Easy does it, Vern. That won't get us very far." He turned to Lorenzo. "Of course, she knew you too. Any reason she was following you around campus this late at night?" he asked.

"I have no idea."

"Sounds to me like you were having a little extracurricular fun with this hot tamale," said Vern sarcastically.

Lorenzo, who rarely resorted to violence even in his teenage years in the *barrio*, hauled off and slugged him in the jaw.

Vern fell to the ground, yelling, "CUFF HIM! CUFF HIM!" He also reached for his gun.

The cop in charge stepped between Vern and Lorenzo. "Put your gun away, Vern." Then he turned to the young cop. "Andy, take him to the car and drive him to the ER—I think he'll live. But first call for the ambulance."

The two walked away, Vern limping and moaning all the way.

The last cop turned to Lorenzo and stuck out his hand. "Dwight King. You know, you shouldn't've slugged him."

"I know. Sorry. Thanks for understanding," said Lorenzo. "I couldn't stand your partner talking about Mrs. Askew that way. I guess I kind of lost it. He is more than a little bit racist."

"Vern is from another era. He retired from the police force in a small town up in the San Joaquin Valley. I'm sure they think every person of Hispanic descent is a member of a gang or in this country illegally. He thinks it's his sworn duty to arrest as many of them as he can."

King paused and then got back to business.

"So, do you know what actually happened here? If you didn't do this, who did?"

Lorenzo just shrugged, deciding that it would be better to keep quiet.

"Well, I guess we'll have to leave this up to the detectives. You'll need to stay here until the ambulance arrives. Do you want to call someone?"

"Yeah, I think I'd better do that. I've met a detective in the LAPD. Her name's Jane Berman. She knows my story, but I won't bore you with it now."

"Okay," said King. "I'm going to get some water—you want some?"

Lorenzo nodded and tried to smile. After King walked away, he pulled out his cell phone and punched in Berman's number. It rang once and she answered.

"You don't even sound sleepy," he said. "Lorenzo Madrid. Sorry for calling so late, but I need your help. I'm in a bit of a jam."

## CHAPTER 40

**LORENZO SAT ON A STONE BENCH** opposite the reflecting pool. King brought him a bottle of water and then threw some kind of shroud over Margarita Askew's body.

It was obvious that the dean's wife had been stalking him, as ridiculous as that seemed. Because of his good looks, Lorenzo had always attracted both men and women. He had scant interest in the latter and had paid little attention to the former since Scott had been killed. But strangers didn't know that and came on to him at times.

As he waited for the ambulance to arrive, he thought about the few interactions he had had with Margarita Askew. She had pulled him into the library the last time he attended a reception at her house. Although he couldn't recall her exact words, they had been fairly explicit. But he hadn't pegged her as a stalker. That time the dean had materialized and whisked her away.

From what George Haller had said at their first meeting, Margarita Askew liked to sleep around. Was Haller one of her early conquests, a man she had eventually cast aside? Or had the seemingly clueless dean actually known that his wife had turned him into a laughingstock among his peers and grown to hate her?

To Lorenzo, these facts made both men suspects in her murder.

"There you are, Lorenzo."

"Detective Berman. I am really glad to see you." He stood up and shook hands with her.

"I live near here, so I called my office and came right over."

Just then, Officer King walked up to them. "Dwight King, campus police. I take it you and Mr. Madrid know each other."

"That's right," she said, showing King her credentials.

She turned to Lorenzo. "Why don't you tell me what happened first. And then you can fill me in on when you arrived, officer."

The three of them sat down on the bench. As they did, an ambulance drove across the plaza and stopped near the pool. Several uniformed officers had cordoned off the area with yellow tape—two other men ducked under the tape and walked up to the body.

"That's the medical examiner, George Brace, and his assistants," explained Berman. "They'll do a preliminary exam—to confirm death and look for the cause—and then take the decedent out of here. The big guy is my partner Ben Chambers."

They all watched as Brace knelt down and touched Margarita's wrist, then put a stethoscope on her chest. He nodded at Berman and began to examine the body.

She turned to King. "I'm assuming this place will be crawling with people in a few hours."

"Yeah, this is kind of the crossroads of upper campus," he said. "There'll be people everywhere."

"And there will go my crime scene. When we find out what kind of bullet killed her, I'll bring a squad in here for a careful search. At this point, we don't even know where the killer was standing."

She turned back to Lorenzo. "From what you said, you were talking to her when she was shot?"

"That's right. I was coming out of that building…" he pointed at Royce Hall, "and someone called my name." Then Lorenzo told her everything that had happened from the time he left the law school to the moment Margarita Askew was shot.

"What happened to her clothes?"

Lorenzo played dumb. "I have no idea."

"Why did you think that whoever was following you was going to hurt you?"

At first, this question exasperated Lorenzo. Berman knew about his run-ins with the drug gang. In his mind, his fear was justified. But maybe she didn't want him to go into all of that in front of the campus policeman. So he played dumb.

"It was pretty late, and I didn't expect to see anyone around," he said. "I guess I was just spooked by the footsteps I heard behind me. Maybe none of this is rational. It's hard to say."

Berman caught the drift of what he was doing and dropped the subject. She turned to Officer King. "Please tell me what happened when you got here."

King went over hearing the gunshot and finding Lorenzo kneeling over the body.

"I understand that one of your officers got into a little scuffle with Mr. Madrid?"

"Not one of my smartest moves," muttered Lorenzo.

"Vern's a redneck, no question about it," King answered. He looked around and lowered his voice. "If I had my way, he'd be out of here. But I don't do the hiring."

"Enough said," Berman replied and turned to Lorenzo. "It really isn't a good idea to slug a cop, no matter how much he deserves it."

Lorenzo nodded. "I pride myself on always being calm when I'm in court, but I did overreact with that guy. Thanks for understanding, Officer King."

"No problem."

Just then, they heard a loud voice coming from behind them.

"WHERE IS SHE? WHERE IS MY BELOVED?"

Looking ashen and sounding very out of breath, Dean Carter Askew rushed into the plaza. He had apparently run up the Janss Steps from the lower part of the campus and was heaving, both from exertion and grief. As the men at the taped-off area stopped him from approaching the body, he cried, "HOW WILL I LIVE WITHOUT MY MARGARITA?"

## CHAPTER 11

"THAT'S THE WOMAN'S HUSBAND," whispered Lorenzo to Berman. "He's dean of the law school."

At Berman's direction, the cops manning the tape barricade let Askew through. She walked over to him, hand extended.

"I understand this woman is your wife."

"LET ME SEE HER!" he shouted. "LET ME TOUCH HER FACE!" He made a lunge for the body but could not pull off the tarp because two of the cops held him back.

Berman stepped closer to him. "This is an active crime scene, sir. I'm going to have to ask you to restrain yourself."

Askew's shoulders were heaving from his heavy sobs and tears were running down his face. Berman handed him a handkerchief and led him over to a bench, away from the reflecting pool.

Suddenly noticing Lorenzo, he said, "Madrid, what are you doing here?" Before Lorenzo could answer, Askew stood up, walked over to him, and grabbed him by the shirt. "Were you one of them? Were you one of those guys she liked to fuck instead of me?"

So George Haller had been right about what he told Lorenzo at that first cocktail party: Mrs. Askew did sleep around. But Lorenzo was surprised that the dean knew and, apparently, put up with her various affairs.

Berman stepped between them and made Askew let go of Lorenzo. She gave him a quizzical look, but Lorenzo shrugged his shoulders noncommittally. Berman took Askew back to the bench.

"I need to ask you where you were when you heard about… this," she gestured toward the body, which was visible now as the medical examiner and his assistants had pulled off the shroud to do their work.

"I was spending the evening at home, catching up on paperwork," Askew said, between sobs. "I was waiting for Margarita to come home."

"And where was she tonight?"

"Having dinner with some of her girlfriends," he said. "She hangs around with several Hispanic women who work on campus. They are all academics and high-level staffers." He glanced around nervously and lowered his voice. "I mean, they aren't maids or cooks."

You hypocritical bastard, thought Lorenzo. Because your wife is wealthy and beautiful and from a certain high level of Spanish society, it was okay to marry her?

"And where did they go?" asked Berman.

"I really don't know," Askew said.

"And how did you happen to arrive here so soon after the incident?"

"I was... taking a walk," sputtered Askew. "I live over there." He pointed to the west. "I often run or walk along the track. It's not far from my home."

He turned to Lorenzo. "You've been there, Madrid. Tell her how close it is."

"It isn't far," said Lorenzo. "I live near him, and I walk to work too."

"So, did you walk along the track tonight? It's pretty late. Aren't you afraid you might get mugged?"

"Not on this campus," answered Askew. "It's very safe. We all felt very safe—until now."

"Tell me what happened next." Berman was persistent.

"I...I...was walking on the track, and I heard a gunshot."

"Where were you when you heard the gunshot?"

"Like I said, down on the track."

"We'd have to get a sound technician to tell us whether a gunshot up here could be heard way down there," she said. "I guess the sound would echo off the walls of the building. I just don't know."

"Well, I know where I was when I heard it!" Askew was getting agitated. "Should I call my attorney?" he asked as his tears began to disappear.

"That's up to you," said Berman. "I'm just trying to establish where you were when you heard the shot."

"What about Madrid?" he said loudly. "I'd like to know what he was doing here!"

Lorenzo started to answer, but Berman stopped him.

"That's part of my investigation too," she said.

At this point, the medical examiner's assistants were lifting Margarita Askew's body onto a gurney and getting ready to roll it to a paneled truck with the words "L.A. County Medical Examiner" painted on the side.

Askew got up and looked at Berman, a pleading look in his eyes. "May I see her?"

Berman hesitated but then relented and probably broke some departmental rule to let him do so, thought Lorenzo.

Askew rushed toward the gurney and unzipped the top of the body bag. He grabbed his wife and started kissing her face repeatedly. The attendants tried to pull him back but failed, and everyone—Askew, Margarita, and the two men—wound up on the ground.

Detective Berman did not look amused.

---

## CECILIA VEGA'S STORY

*I didn't have many toys when I was growing up, but I did have a Barbie doll. It was as blond and fair-skinned as I was dark-haired with brown skin. I played with her every day after school, after I had done my homework.*

*My father was long gone, and sometimes my mother brought strange men home at night.*

*I really had to concentrate on my doll then, with all the weird sounds coming from the bedroom.*

*When my grandma found out what my mother was doing, she came one day and told me to pack my clothes and toys. She took me to her house, and I lived with her from then on. I never saw my mother again.*

*Soon after I went to live with my grandma, she told me that I had a brother. I guess his father was one of the many guys my mother had been with. My grandma told me that he was going to take care of me for a few days while she visited her sister who had been sick.*

*I liked Jaime right away. He got me up in the morning for school, gave me breakfast, and fixed my lunch. He picked me up and made dinner for me. He even made sure I did my homework.*

*Jaime was good to me.*

*One day we did not go home when he picked me up from school. He said we had to go to another place for a little while because he had to do what he called "some business" with a man he called a "bad hombre."*

*We drove to a terrible place, an old house not far from our neighborhood. He said it was too dangerous for me to stay in the car so he took me inside with him. He shoved me into a room and ran up the stairs.*

*It smelled funny, and there were people lying around on the floor on dirty mattresses. They looked like they were dead. A few looked at me with glassy eyes and then went back to sleep or back to shooting something into their arms.*

*I could tell that this was a bad place, and I wanted to get out of there, but I had to wait for my brother. So I started playing with my Barbie, which I always kept in my backpack.*

*After a while, I heard shouts from upstairs and outside. Then I heard loud noises and banging on the door. In a minute or so, the door kind of disintegrated and a bunch of police wearing helmets and strange clothes rushed into the room. A nice lady policeman saw me and led me out the door and into her car. They called my grandma, and she picked me up in a few hours.*

*I never saw my brother again.*

## CHAPTER 42

**AFTER NESTOR AND SAUL LEFT THE ROOM,** Pantera yawned and walked into one of the side rooms where Felix had put a bed. Without closing the door, he started taking off his clothes. Perez glanced in his direction then moved to another part of the room.

"Not bad, eh?" Pantera said, as he reappeared at the door, completely naked. "You can see why the *señoritas* like to spend time with me."

Just then, Felix walked into the room with two young women by his side. To Perez, they looked to be in their teens, at best. They were giggling as they disappeared into the room with Pantera. Then he closed the door.

Felix walked over to Perez and sat down at the table.

"How do you take it?" asked Perez. "I mean, that guy is *loco—mucho loco.*" He pointed to his head.

Felix glanced around the room nervously before speaking. With just the two of them there, Perez hoped the younger man would feel free to talk.

"It is very hard sometimes," Felix said with a sigh. "He has me do things for him that I don't want to do. But what choice do I have?"

"What do you mean?" asked Perez. "You can run away and lose yourself in the *barrio* of a big city, far away from here and from Mexico."

"He would hunt me down like a dog," said Felix, shivering slightly at the thought. "I know too much."

"What do you mean? About his whole operation?"

"*Sí,* and all the bad things he has done in the last year. He has had many people killed and killed some himself. You saw what he did to that guy who failed you."

"Hugo," said Perez, shaking his head. "That shocked me, and I'm not easily shocked. He was dumb, but he didn't deserve that."

"*Señor* Pantera calls that '*justicia.*'"

"Some 'justice.' How did you get mixed up with him?"

"He came to my village about five years ago and kind of bought me from my parents," said Felix. "They were poor and, with eight other kids, it was a relief to get rid of one—me!"

"Why did he single you out?" asked Perez. "There are so many kids in all the villages in Mexico, many who look just like you. Why you, I wonder?"

"He's got connections all over central Mexico, including some priests who are on his payroll. At least, that's what he told me once, when he was drunk. The priest in our village told him how well I did in school, and he just marched into town one day with about ten of his guys and took me away. As he led me from our house, he threw some money at my father. I will never forget how I felt when my father did not even look at me because he was so eager to pick up the money. My mother was crying, and so were my little brothers and sisters, but that was all. I was taken from there, and I know I will never return."

"What happened next?"

"He took me to Cancun and enrolled me in a Catholic school. I didn't see him for a couple of years. I was happy there and learned a lot. He insisted that I study math, business, and law, which I did. Then one day, out of nowhere, one of his men came to get me and poof! I was gone. And I've been trailing him around ever since, doing whatever he asks me to do. So far, that has not included killing someone. He says he needs me for my brain."

"But I still think you should run away," said Perez. "Hell, I'd help you."

"Help him do what?" asked Pantera, who stood naked in the doorway, scratching his testicles.

## CHAPTER 13

**DETECTIVE BERMAN ORDERED ONE OF HER MEN** to drive Askew home when he was finally untangled from his wife's body and the two attendants. The scene fascinated Lorenzo, who was still sitting on the bench by the fountain. This was a side of the law he didn't usually witness. Berman walked over to him as the medical examiner and his men loaded Mrs. Askew's body into the panel truck.

"You're very calm," she said, sitting down next to Lorenzo. "Aren't you upset?"

"Look, detective. I've been to crime scenes and seen bodies before. This is nothing new to me."

"But someone you knew is dead, shot almost in front of you," she said.

"I barely knew her. I've only seen her twice since I moved to L.A."

"But she seemed to know you . . . or wanted to know you," said Berman. "I mean, it looks to me like she was stalking you."

"News to me," said Lorenzo.

"Are you sure you're telling me everything?" she asked. "You're a handsome guy, and from what I saw of her husband, much better looking than him. She never came on to you?"

Lorenzo thought for a moment before answering. "Just once, at a faculty gathering at their house a couple of weeks ago," he said. "It was harmless. As I was walking down the hall, she grabbed my arm and pulled me into a room."

"What did you think?" asked Berman. "More importantly, what did you do?"

"It scared the hell out of me."

"What did she say?"

"She said something about wanting to get to know me better."

"I'll bet she did." Berman laughed. "And then what?"

"Before I could react, another faculty member walked into the room and rescued me. And the dean walked in right behind her."

"And what did Mrs. Askew do?"

Lorenzo cringed. "She looked angry."

"And you did not see her after that?"

"Not until tonight."

Neither of them said anything for a few minutes.

"I think we need to get you home," Berman finally said. "I'll send someone by your house to get your formal statement tomorrow. Under the circumstances, I won't make you come to the station. Because I already knew about the gangbangers, it makes perfect sense that you'd be afraid when you discovered that someone was following you. I'm going to concentrate on what Mrs. Askew was doing before she came to campus to follow you."

"Let me know if I can help in any way," said Lorenzo.

Berman laughed and waved her hand dismissively. "We don't let amateurs anywhere near our cases."

She signaled to one of the cops who had been guarding the crime scene. "Take the good professor home," she said, as she turned to watch the technicians taking photos and looking for evidence. "I'll be in touch," she said over her shoulder.

## CHAPTER 44

IF PANTERA FELT HE LOOKED LIKE some kind of Aztec god, Perez did not share that sentiment. It revolted him to see this maniac strutting around without clothes. And he was equally angry that Pantera had had sex with young women who were barely old enough to even be capable of having sex. That was something he would never do. He had been with many whores, but he drew the line at young ones like these two.

"Help him do what?" repeated Pantera.

"Improve his English," said Perez, thinking fast.

Felix looked relieved.

Pantera yawned, stretched, and scratched his testicles again. "His English sounds good to me," he said. "No need for that kind of lesson. He needs my kind of lesson. How to become a killer like me. He needs to be so bad that everyone is afraid of him!" Then he threw back his head and laughed loudly. "You could never do that, I know. But I need you to keep track of my business interests and my personal shit. Okay, little *amigo?*"

"*Sí, sí, Señor* Pantera," said Felix. "I am here only to serve you."

Perez nearly gagged at those words, but he knew Felix had no choice—he had to grovel.

Pantera turned to Perez. "What is your plan to get that bastard Madrid here, where I can deal with him directly? No one seems to be able to do that simple thing." He started poking a finger in Perez's chest. "I WANT HIM HERE, SO I CAN LOOK HIM IN THE EYES WHEN I SLIT HIS THROAT!"

"I have a plan. I'll tell you about it when we no longer have visitors." Perez motioned toward the door of the bedroom where the two girls were now standing, also naked.

When Pantera turned to look at them, he seemed surprised to see them. "You girls can get dressed," he said and threw some money at them. He watched them scramble for the floating bills, then shouted, "Now, get the fuck out of my sight!"

When the two girls had left by the front door, Pantera sauntered into the bedroom and emerged wearing pants tucked into his boots and a long canvas coat. He turned to Perez.

"So where are your so-called men? Why all this delay? I need Madrid now! I thought they had him cornered in that legal office. You said the place was surrounded. How did he get away?"

Perez was seething mad that Pantera was second-guessing him, but he kept his voice steady. "They said there were too many people around there to do anything," he said. "Too many of our people. It is in the *barrio, señor*. Any sign of trouble, and the cops will be all over us." Time to grovel a bit himself. "If you will wait for another day, I can guarantee that we will find Lorenzo Madrid and bring him here for you to deal with. It is time for me to take charge."

Pantera was studying his fingernails. "I will give you one more day," he said. "After that, I will bring in more of my guys, and they won't fail me."

"I will be most grateful," said Perez, practically gritting his teeth. "I'm leaving now to meet with my men."

But Perez had no intention of meeting his men. He had decided to handle the capture of Lorenzo Madrid himself. But before that, he needed to drop by his apartment.

## CHAPTER 15

**EVEN THOUGH HE WAS NOT SCHEDULED** to take the students to the clinic until later in the day, Lorenzo got up early and walked to campus. After what he had been through, he needed time to think. The stroll through his upscale neighborhood and onto the campus gave him time to think about the bizarre events of the night before.

First, Margarita Askew stalking him and then getting shot in the process? He shook his head in disbelief.

Then, the dean's question about him being one of her lovers—mindboggling!

Finally, would what the dean said mean that he would be fired?

He shook his head as he recalled all that had happened. He had had no romantic interest in the dean's wife, nor had he acted in any way that would have given her that impression. He had not let himself get involved with anyone, man or woman, since Scott was murdered before his eyes those many years ago.

"I dedicate myself to my work," he often said to anyone who expressed any interest in him sexually. And he had done that for years. Of course, he couldn't go into all of that with the police or anyone else—he doubted they would truly understand.

As he started to walk up the Janss Steps into the central part of the UCLA campus, it suddenly occurred to him that he had to talk this over with Leslie Mason. They had chatted frequently since they met, and he considered her a friend.

When he reached the top of the steps, the scene of the crime lay before him. The blood on the bricks had been cleaned up and the police tape around the fountain removed, but after what had happened here, he found it hard to look at.

Lorenzo walked along the plaza, barely noticing the people he passed. He entered the law school building and walked straight to the dean's office. He hoped that Miss Stein would bring him up to date.

As he walked up to her door, he saw that she was on the phone, so he waited outside for to finish her call.

For some strange reason, Miss Stein had put the caller on speaker, and Lorenzo distinctly heard a man on the other end ask, "Is this the law school at the university?"

"Yes, it is, but you have reached the dean's office," said Miss Stein. "What did you want—maybe I can transfer your call."

"Well . . . er . . . this is Mr. Baker. I'm the brother of an old school friend of the dean's wife. I was in town, and she asked me . . ."

Miss Stein's answer was both cold and precise. "I am afraid that would be impossible."

"And why is that?" The man's tone had changed. Lorenzo could tell he was becoming agitated. "I need to get in touch with her as soon as possible because I am leaving . . ."

"How many times do I have to tell you, Mr. Baker? That is impossible."

"Listen, you..."

"I'm sorry Mr. Baker, but you will have to relay the news to your sister that Mrs. Askew is dead."

There was a stunned silence for a moment, and then the man let out a loud scream and the phone went dead.

Miss Stein noticed that Lorenzo was at her door, and she invited him in. Then, not realizing that he had heard the man on the phone, she relayed the conversation to Lorenzo. "How odd. Someone was trying to reach Mrs. Askew and hadn't heard about her death. A brother of an old friend, he said. When I told him the news, he screamed and dropped the phone. There was a loud crash and the line went dead."

She paused and then said, "It was very strange."

She thought a moment more and looked again at Lorenzo.

"Professor Madrid. I'm sorry to be so preoccupied. You have been through a terrible ordeal. I was so sorry to hear about it. Sit down, please."

Lorenzo had never seen this side of Miss Stein. Her icy personality had a soft side after all. And he was glad to have the benefit of it, especially at this stressful time. Executive secretaries run the world, and those who ignore them or treat them condescendingly live to regret it.

"Yeah, it was pretty crazy," he said. "It happened so fast. I didn't..."

"I heard that you were walking back from campus and went into Royce Hall?"

"Yes, that's right."

"And Mrs. Askew was there too?"

Lorenzo didn't really want to talk about Margarita Askew at all. "Not with me, but I guess she happened to be outside when she was killed."

"Needless to say, the whole thing is very strange. I wonder why she was walking on campus so late?"

Stalking me, thought Lorenzo. But he only shrugged.

"Anyway, the dean is not here, if you wondered about him. He is under a doctor's care at home, but someone called to say that he might be moved to the medical center later today." She looked around conspiratorially. "Psych ward is where he should be," she whispered. "That woman gave him no end of trouble. Was driving him slowly crazy. Having sex with any man wearing pants! Outrageous! I imagine that man who just called was one of her lovers. Brother of a friend, my eye!"

Lorenzo found this very interesting but couldn't let on that he did. "I feel bad about everything. I wondered if it will affect the school in any way. I mean, with the dean so incapacitated."

"I shouldn't think so. Professor Mason has been serving as associate dean, and if the dean has to step down, she will be able to handle the job very well. Do you know Professor Mason?"

"Yes, I do. We met at the first faculty reception I went to, and we've had chats many times." He looked at the neat stacks of folders on her desk. "I see that you've got better things to do than talk to me. Thank you for your time and the information. If I can do anything to help you in this difficult time, please let me know. I'll tell Professor Mason the same."

※ ※ ※

After putting his briefcase in his office, Lorenzo walked to Leslie Mason's door. He heard yelling from down the hall but decided he had more important things on his mind and ignored it.

"Come in," she said from inside.

When he walked in and she saw who it was, she got up from her chair and walked over and hugged him.

"God, man. You've sure been through the mill. Sit down and tell me about it."

## CHAPTER 46

"YOU LOOK LIKE HELL," Leslie said. "Did you sleep at all last night?"

"Not very well. You heard about what happened? I mean, the whole sordid story?"

"I only know that Margarita Askew was shot and you were nearby," she said. "And the dean got there and had some kind of breakdown."

"Yeah, that's the abbreviated version, I suppose for public consumption," he answered, shaking his head ruefully. "Have you got time to hear all of this?"

"Yes, yes. I need to hear it. I'm free all morning."

He told her about walking through campus and deciding that someone was following him and going into Royce Hall to get away.

"But why would anyone be following you? This campus is very safe and heavily patrolled at all hours. I work here at night often and walk to my car—I've never had a problem in five years."

Leslie was reverting to the good lawyer she was, but Lorenzo wasn't ready to answer all of her questions. He still feared that the problems that had followed him from Oregon would impact his new life here.

"Let's just say that some bad people in Oregon were pretty mad at me over a case, and I worry that they might follow me here."

"A drug case, I presume?"

"Yeah, it was. But it's a long story, and I won't bore you with it now. Maybe sometime later."

"So you ducked into Royce Hall to get away?"

"I did, and after a while I decided that either I was imagining it or whoever was after me had left. So I walked outside through a back door and was getting ready to run down the path to lower campus when someone called my name. I ran back toward that small reflecting pool at the end of the plaza where the sound seemed to have come from and saw a figure standing by the water. It turned out to be Mrs. Askew. A few seconds later, I heard a shot, and she fell forward into the water. I pulled her out and was giving her CPR when the police arrived and all hell broke loose." By the time he finished telling his story, Lorenzo's throat was very dry and his stomach was churning.

Leslie could tell he wasn't feeling well, so she poured him a glass of water and handed it to him. He emptied the glass in one long gulp.

"Thanks. That tasted good. I needed something to clear my throat."

"You know, Lorenzo, you might be in some kind of shock over this," she said. "Have you been to a doctor?"

"No, I don't think I need to do that. I've seen lots of bad stuff in my career. This just happened so fast, with no warning. I didn't expect anything like it to happen."

Professor Mason nodded knowingly and said, "No one did, but Margarita might have brought it on herself by sleeping around, and I don't mean with just one or two guys. I mean a lot of guys. And some got hurt because they slept with her. Let's start with George Haller. He used to be a nice guy until he spent a night or two with her at a legal meeting in New York a year or so ago. He fell for her, big time, and he told me that she even said she would leave the dean for him. Fat chance, but he believed her. And when she dumped him, she convinced the dean that he should not get promoted . . . so he wasn't. And one of your own students: the Native American kid, Asa Lone Eagle."

"Asa? She slept with Asa?" He shook his head in disbelief. "She was a monster!"

"Smart, handsome kid, fresh off the reservation somewhere. He gets to the big city and crosses paths with her, and before you know it, she's rented a hotel room. And she did this with more than one student! In his case, he dumped her. I guess he realized that it was not a good idea to be messing around with the dean's wife, so he told her. She flew into a rage and tried to get his scholarship money cut off."

"Poor dumb kid," said Lorenzo.

"I'm chair of the scholarship committee so I blocked that from happening," she said.

"But he still works at the house when they have parties," said Lorenzo.

"I guess he needs the money," said Leslie. "I've seen her look daggers at him when he's serving, but he ignores her. And I suppose she had long ago moved on to someone else."

Lorenzo shook his head in dismay.

"And she certainly had her eyes on you," she said. "I could tell that night I rescued you after she dragged you into the library."

"Yeah, I remember. You saved me, but I just thought it was some harmless flirting. I get hit on from time to time—I'm used to it."

"I'm not surprised. You are very good looking." She laughed. "She even asked me if you were married."

"No, not even close," he said firmly.

"Well, she had apparently set her sights on you and was not ready to take no for an answer."

"I wonder what she'd have done if I had gone along with her?" he wondered out loud.

"Drawn and quartered and hogtied you and had you delivered to her bedroom, I'd guess."

That remark relieved some of the tension so they could even laugh a little.

## CHAPTER 47

**BEFORE HE MADE THE CALL** to the law school, Perez drove to his apartment in Silver Lake and changed into his "workman" clothes: brown shirt and pants and a cap with a UCLA logo on the front. Parked next to his Cadillac in the garage was a vehicle he drove when he wanted to be inconspicuous: a 1990 Nissan pickup that hadn't been washed in over a year.

No one would notice him when he entered what he considered "enemy" territory—the west side of Los Angeles where much of the wealth of the area was concentrated. He hoped that no one would pay attention to him on the UCLA campus. He would look like just another worker, sweeping streets and dumping trash.

A week ago, he had paid one of the regular grounds crew to get him an official shirt with the UCLA logo on one side of the front and the name "Juan" on the other. He also asked for a university ID card. If anyone challenged him, he would only have to produce the card, point to the front of the shirt, bow, and say *"No Inglés."* He could bluff his way through anything.

Perez did not intend to confront Madrid on campus. His aim was to follow him to a place where he could grab him and take him to Boyle Heights and Pantera. That maniac would not believe him if he merely said that Madrid had been eliminated. It had to be done in front of Pantera, who would probably like to watch it anyway, sadist that he was.

After he parked his truck at the campus, Perez called his sister's cell, a number he had been ordered never to call. He knew his sister was married to the dean, so maybe he could convince her to tell him about Madrid and the legal clinic in Boyle Heights.

He made the call and then, after being transferred to the dean's office, a woman there told him that his sister was dead. He had always prided himself in his ability to remain cool when he was under pressure, and this was definitely the time to show that control. Although he had not seen his sister in years and doubted she thought much about him, he was upset and shed a few tears as he thought about her and wondered how she had died.

But there was no time for mourning now. He had a job to do. He squared his shoulders, dried his eyes, and got out of the truck.

Perez joined a group of workers as they walked to their various assigned tasks for the day. No one paid attention to him, thinking that he was just a new guy brought in to help the regular crew. When they reached the law school, Perez veered off and started raking the dirt in some flower beds close to the main door.

After a few minutes of this boring job, he started sweeping the walkway. Various men and women walked in and out of the building, and everyone ignored him. As a stranger in a strange land, he was used to that, but it still galled him to be so rudely ignored. He **was** someone who mattered. He was a successful businessman who made more money than any of these people would ever dream of!

Eventually, a nice-looking Hispanic man walked toward the building and nodded to Perez. Courtesy mattered to Perez, so he muttered a greeting, *"Buenos diás, señor."* As the man walked on, the face in the photo he had been circulating to his men flashed into his mind. This was Lorenzo Madrid!

Perez kept sweeping for a few seconds and then, throwing caution and his broom aside, he followed Madrid into the building. He could see down the long hallway that Madrid was going through a door at the other end. Playing his part, he picked up a small trash can from inside the door and pretended to be looking for other cans to empty as he walked down the hall.

The door at the end of the hall was marked "Carter Askew, Office of the Dean." He contemplated walking in, but decided that was too risky. Instead, he walked along to another door marked "Janitor" and stepped inside, where he found brooms and mops and a sink. He decided to wait there while he figured out what to do. He kept opening the door a crack in order to watch for Madrid.

After several minutes, the door of the room opened and an older Hispanic woman stepped inside. When she saw him, she began screaming at the top of her lungs, *"Socorro! Socorro!* Help! Help!"

## CHAPTER 48

**LORENZO WENT TO HIS OFFICE** after meeting with Leslie Mason. Even though it was hard to concentrate on work, given what had happened the night before, he managed to jot down a few things he wanted to tell the students when they got there at eleven.

He had talked with Victoria at the clinic about making another visit, and she had agreed. She expected them at two to continue their study of the files and to sit in on several client interviews. He was pleased that his plans for the TAs were working out, in spite of all the things that had happened.

His TAs all arrived at his office within minutes of one another. His office had room for a small library table and four chairs. He wheeled over the one behind his desk and motioned for all of them to sit down.

Alex placed a copy of the *Daily Bruin* in front of Lorenzo. "You've known me long enough to realize that I speak my mind, Professor Madrid. So I have to ask, and excuse my vulgar language, but what's up with this shit? You involved in a shooting on campus? I gotta ask, and you gotta be straight with us!"

With everything so chaotic and uncertain, Lorenzo had dodged the calls from the *Daily Bruin* reporter early this morning. He decided it was best to keep quiet publicly about what had happened, given the police investigation and his own uncertain status at the university. But these kids needed to hear something from him. They needed to hear that he had been an innocent victim in the events of the night before.

"I need you to not say anything to anyone about what I'm going to tell you," he began. "When you are all practicing law, you will have to keep everything a client tells you to yourself. No exceptions. In this case, just consider me your client."

They all nodded.

He gave them a brief synopsis of what had happened, leaving out any mention of the possibility that Margarita Askew had been following him, perhaps even stalking him. He also simplified the story, skipping the part about her disrobing and trying to kiss him, for the benefit of the kids.

"You found her body?" asked Asa, with a sad look in his eyes. Lorenzo hoped he hadn't been ruined for life by his encounter with the shameless Margarita Askew.

"Yes, after I heard someone shouting near that reflecting pool in front of Royce Hall. I walked over to it and then heard a shot. I rushed to the person who had been shot and recognized Mrs. Askew. I pulled her out of the water, but she was dead."

"God, that's awful," said Cecilia. "You poor man."

"And poor her," said Nathan.

"Yeah, of course, I should have said so," said Cecilia.

"So the police are investigating and looking for the killer, and I'm trying to go on with my life here. And my life here involves the four of you. Victoria Ramos has agreed to let us visit the clinic again, and she's expecting us at two. Let's talk about what you'll encounter when you meet some of her clients. And I want to answer any questions you have."

After an hour of a good back-and-forth discussion, Lorenzo held up his hand.

"I'm impressed with the depth of your preparation and your knowledge. I think we should have lunch—my treat—on the way to the clinic."

The four students exchanged smiles and packed up their stuff. Then Lorenzo led them to the parking garage, and they got into a university van for the drive to downtown.

↟ ↟ ↟

Their destination was Philippe's, a venerable Los Angeles restaurant near Union Station. Lorenzo loved this place and even knew its history.

It had first opened its doors in another location in 1908. The owner, Philippe Mathieu, claimed to have invented the French dip sandwich one day when, by accident, he dropped a sliced French roll into the roasting pan filled with juice still hot from the oven. People liked the taste and a new kind of sandwich was born.

Lorenzo loved the story and liked the sandwiches and the atmosphere even more. As they had done for years, customers lined up at the long counter, placed their orders (cash only), then watched the "carvers" make the sandwiches. Lorenzo loved their beef French dip sandwiches and coleslaw, but there were also ham, turkey, pork, and even lamb dip sandwiches.

The place was the least pretentious restaurant in town, but the food had always been the drawing card here. When he lived in L.A., Lorenzo had often seen people in evening clothes sitting at the long wooden tables next to skid row bums.

Lorenzo snagged a table and stepped up to the counter to place their orders. He was soon joined in the line by Asa.

"You need some help carrying our food, sir?"

"Yes, that would be great."

They made small talk for a while and then Asa said, "I'm really sorry about Mrs. Askew, I mean her being dead and all."

"I didn't know her all that well," said Lorenzo. Not as well as you apparently did, he thought to himself.

"She was really nice to me and kept hiring me to serve at the house when they had parties, you know like the ones you attended? She did a lot to help me."

"That was nice of her," said Lorenzo. But what about her trying to screw up your scholarship, he thought.

"Here you go, sir," said the lady behind the counter. "I hope you and your son enjoy the sandwiches."

Lorenzo and Asa exchanged laughs and carried the two trays to the table. The meal was pleasant, with no talk of death or dying or even the law.

None of them noticed the Mexican man dressed in work clothes, sitting at a nearby table within ear shot. Esteban Perez pretended to be concentrating on his sandwich and his beer, but he was listening to every word.

## CHAPTER 19

**AS THEY LEFT PHILIPPE'S,** Lorenzo began to feel sick. When he put his hand on his forehead, it felt hot. He even felt a bit dizzy. When they got to the van, he motioned for the four students to gather round.

"You know, I don't feel very well," he told them. He was touched by the looks of concern on their faces. "But I think all of you should go to the clinic. I'll call Victoria Ramos, and tell her you're on the way. I'm sure things are all set up for you to work there this afternoon, and I don't want to disappoint you."

He turned to Asa. "You told me you worked at jobs all around campus. Does that mean you're able to drive university vehicles?"

"Yes, sir. I do it all the time." He pulled a card out of his wallet and showed it to Lorenzo.

"Would you want to do that right now?"

"I could, sure. Happy to do that."

Lorenzo looked at the others. "Okay with the rest of you if Asa is your driver today?"

They nodded.

"How will you get home?" asked Cecilia.

"I'll walk across the street and get a cab." He motioned toward Union Station, which was visible several blocks away.

"At least let us drop you off at the station," said Asa.

"Good idea," said Lorenzo.

So they got into the van, and Asa drove up to the main doors of the station.

When Lorenzo got out, he said, "Have a good day. I'll call Victoria now, and tell her about the change in plans." He waved as the van pulled away.

Turning around, he was relieved to see a whole line of cab drivers waiting their turns to pick up passengers walking out of the station. He called the clinic and talked to Ronaldo Soto because Victoria was meeting with clients.

He was back at his house in Westwood in an hour and a half.

※ ※ ※

Lorenzo woke up at about 8 p.m., feeling a bit better physically. His mental state was another story, however. When he got up to get a glass of water, the old sense of fear and depression hit him.

If he thought about it, that was not surprising, given what he had been through in the desert earlier that year: being threatened with death by the drug gang, his escape, and the fear that had caused him, then the murder of his neighbor who was mistaken for him and the worry that he was in danger here. And, there were the other more recent occurrences. It was all catching up with him. Did he have PTSD? He hadn't sought professional help before, but maybe he needed to.

Throwing himself into his work had been his catharsis in the past, ever since Scott had been killed. When the hopelessness hit him those last months in Oregon, he decided to move. Now, here he was in a new situation that he liked, and he was once again afraid and depressed. Of course, he had good reason. He had just seen someone shot right in front of him. Was the bullet meant for him?

Although he had kept it at bay for a long time, here it was, like a demon perched on his shoulder. He vowed to see a psychiatrist soon. But what about now, what about tonight? He needed a release. Tonight, a cold shower would not work. Shivering slightly, he put on the flashy clothes he never wore anymore and headed out the door.

## CHAPTER 50

**WEST HOLLYWOOD HAD BEEN A MECCA** for gay men as long as Lorenzo could remember. He had gone there as a scared teenager when he was still in high school. Because he was handsome, he attracted the attention of men of all ages, but he had been too frightened to do anything more than look. Later in college, he had gone a bit farther and done things in back rooms that he was not proud of.

After he met Scott, he didn't go to West Hollywood again. The AIDS crisis kept him away as well. In the years since, he had been content to become, as he told anyone who asked, "as celibate as a priest." However, given the recent scandals in the church involving priests and altar boys, that phrase was probably not very accurate these days.

Lorenzo parked his car on a side street and walked over to Santa Monica Boulevard, where most of the action he was looking for took place. With his dark good looks, slim body, and the tight-fitting clothes he was wearing, he figured he would be able to achieve his goal for the night: to have sex with enough men to purge the demons from his soul.

As melodramatic as that seemed, Lorenzo knew that strategy would work. He had hidden his homosexuality for years—first from his parents, then during most of the time in college and law school, and later from the people he worked with and for at his law office. The *macho* nature of Mexican culture would render him useless as an advocate for his clients if they even suspected the truth about him. The very people he worked so many hours to help would shun him if they knew his secret. It was better to repress his urges and stay focused on his work.

Tonight was different though. For reasons even he did not totally understand, he had to do what he was about to do. He walked into the Gold Coast, the first bar he saw, and stood in the doorway. He knew every eye in the place was on him as he walked to the bar and ordered a drink.

A muscular blond guy approached him first.

"You alone, honey?"

"Until now," Lorenzo said, knowing what was coming next.

"You're pretty hot for an older guy. Anyone ever tell you that you look like Antonio Banderas?"

"Yeah, a few times," said Lorenzo, taking a sip of his margarita.

"But he's looking a bit old around the edges," said blondie. "And he got married to that Melanie what's-her-name. Not too cool a move." He turned to another blond who had sat down on the other side of Lorenzo. "Hey, Freddie, who does this delicious hunk remind you of?"

The second blond, more effeminate-looking than the first, looked closely at Lorenzo's face.

"Gol, baby, I'm not sure. Maybe the guy who used to do those Chrysler car commercials I saw on TV when I was a little kid." He thought for a moment and came up with an answer. "Ricardo Monta-something."

"Montalbán," said Lorenzo. "He was Latin, and he was old like me."

"Oh, honey," said the first blond, "age is no barrier when true love comes along. I'd be willing to take a chance with you."

Lorenzo smiled and said, "But you'd still be worrying that I might die of a heart attack while we were, you know, going at it. I don't think so. But thanks."

Walking away from the blonds and their laughter, Lorenzo found an empty table and sat down. The table felt sticky when he touched it, so he hailed a waitress.

"Could you wipe this off for me? It's really sticky."

"Sure, honey," said the older waitress, who could probably write a book about the things she'd seen in her time working here. "You look too high class to be cruising in here."

"Thanks for the compliment, I think," he smiled and ordered another drink. He gave her a five-dollar bill.

"I'll be right back with your drink," she said.

Lorenzo looked around the room at the mass of bronzed and well-toned bodies. Not an ugly guy in the place, he thought to himself.

"Mind if I join you?"

Ronaldo Soto from the legal clinic sat down opposite him.

## CHAPTER 51

**LORENZO HAD TALKED TO SOTO ONLY BRIEFLY** at the clinic because he usually met with Victoria. As the man sat across from him, Lorenzo looked at him more closely. He was probably in his late thirties. His skin was lighter than Lorenzo's, and he had fine, almost feminine, features. He was dressed for the office: a suit and white shirt. His tie, which had tiny sombreros on it, was loose at this throat.

"I guess this is where I say that I'm surprised to see you in a place like this," he said.

Lorenzo would never deny his sexual preferences, but the subject was usually not something he brought up when there was no reason to do so.

"I'd say the same about you, Ronaldo," he said.

"If you're keeping this a secret, I understand," he said. "I never saw you here . . ." he glanced around the room, "if you never saw me."

"Of course," said Lorenzo. "But I think society has reached the point where I—and I presume you—don't have to hide what we are. Does Victoria know?"

Soto sighed. "Yeah, she does, and she doesn't care. As long as I don't hit on the young guys we help." He looked around. "Not that I would. I presume it's the way you operate around your male clients and your law students."

Lorenzo looked around the room and nodded his head. "Yes, of course. I haven't been in a place like this for years. Being gay doesn't bother me. I've lived with my deep dark secret for most of my adult life, and I have accepted it. But being in a place like this, with all this wanton sexuality on display, kind of sickens me."

"So why did you come here?" asked Soto, finishing a beer and signaling for another.

"Why indeed," said Lorenzo, with a sigh. He paused. Should he say what he was about to say to someone he barely knew? What the hell, he reasoned. Why not? "I felt like I needed the kind of release I can get only from sex with another man."

Soto smiled and waved to two men who were headed for the table. "Have I got a deal for you." He introduced both men as they sat down.

One was his lover, Peter Mathews, a medical resident at USC County General Hospital. The other young man was Victor Ruez, an attorney who had just started his own practice.

Mathews was short like Soto, with red hair and the pale skin to go with it. He and Soto were nice contrasts. Ruez was tall and slim like Lorenzo, but with the rugged look of a man who spent his time working outdoors on a dock or in a factory, not a courtroom. He was good looking enough to attract the attention of the forward-acting gay guys who paraded by the table constantly.

The four made small talk for an hour or so, about their lives and their plans. Three drinks later, Soto and Mathews stood up.

"We've got to get going," Soto said. "We always finish our date in a certain way."

Mathews blushed.

"In his bed or mine," continued Soto. "You two have fun."

Lorenzo looked at Ruez. "I guess I should do the same, I mean leave."

"You don't look like you are in any condition to drive," Ruez said. "Although I work in East L.A., I live near here. Keeps me near the action, if I want it. I've got a nice soft couch, and you're welcome to use it tonight."

"Part of me wants to refuse your offer, but the other part says I should go home with you. That part is winning. Let's go."

※ ※ ※

After several hours of very good sex, Lorenzo fell asleep with his body entwined with Victor's. For the first time in a long time, he felt the demons that had been plaguing him drain away.

His cell phone woke him up at 2:30 a.m.

"Lorenzo? It's Victoria." She sounded strange.

"Victoria. What's wrong?"

"You need to come to the clinic."

"What's happened? You sound afraid. . . ."

There was silence on the other end for a moment, then someone else took the phone.

"Lorenzo Madrid." The voice was low and menacing. "You need to come to your old place of business."

Lorenzo was confused. "What do you mean? I have no place of business in L.A. Who are you?"

"Pardon me," said the voice. "I mean your father's old place of business. The nursery. I should add that you need to come here if you want to see your precious students again. I'll give you two hours, *maricón!*"

The phone went dead. Lorenzo jumped out of bed and put on his clothes, pausing only to kiss a bewildered Victor as he raced out the door.

"I'll try to call you later," he said over his shoulder. "And thanks. You saved me."

## CHAPTER 52

EARLIER THAT DAY, Victoria Ramos was waiting just inside the door for the four students as they drove up to the clinic.

"Come in, come in," she said, shaking hands with all of them and gesturing for them to follow her into the back.

*"Un momento, por favor,"* she said over her shoulder to the people sitting in the anteroom.

"How is Professor Madrid?" she asked, as they sat down around the table in the conference room. She filled four cups with coffee as she waited for an answer.

"He looked pretty green around the gills," said Alex.

"Kind of pale," added Nathan.

"I hope he's feeling better," said Cecilia.

"Cream and sugar are over on the table," Victoria said to them. "Or, if you prefer tea, there's hot water in the thermos and tea bags in the glass jar." She sat down and looked at each of them. "In a large city like this one, all kinds of illnesses are in the air. He'll be fine, I'm sure."

She sipped her coffee, and the four students took that as a cue to do the same.

"So, what are we going to do today?" asked Alex, as always the most forward.

"Lorenzo . . . Mr. Madrid thought you should have a real taste of what we do here at the clinic by hearing the stories of some of the clients I work with," she said.

They all smiled and nodded.

"So, I'm going to bring you into the meetings with three of my regular clients tonight. You can listen and take notes, but I don't want you to say anything to them unless I tell you it's okay to do so. I need to keep some control over this. In the meantime, you can work on your notes and read their files. I've got some case law to have you review too."

"Is that permitted under bar association rules?" asked Nathan, the most careful of the four.

"Is what permitted under bar association rules?" asked Victoria.

"Letting us meet with your clients and read about their legal problems."

"You are my legal interns," she said. "I'm allowed to do this kind of thing for educational purposes, as long as I have the permission of the clients involved. And I do."

She looked intently at the students. "I need you to promise me that you will follow that rule about waiting until I say it's okay to ask questions. Professor Madrid tells me that you are all eager to learn but that some of you like to talk a lot."

She looked directly at Alex.

"That would apply to me," he said with a laugh. "I plead guilty."

The others laughed, too.

"Growing up where I did, I couldn't have survived without speaking my mind and standing up for myself," he said. "From what my friends here have told me about their backgrounds, I don't think anything will surprise us. We are all survivors."

Victoria nodded and said, "I grew up like that too." She smiled and stood up. "Wait here for a moment while I get things organized."

As soon as she walked out the door, the students were abuzz.

"This will be ideal for us," said Nathan, in his formal and dignified way.

"I've always wanted to help my people," said Cecilia. "I'm really happy about this chance."

"Maybe I can right some of the wrongs done to my people," said Asa.

"Shit, you guys," said Alex, "you are all so high-minded. We need to find the answer to the most pressing question of all: are Victoria and Professor M getting it on? I mean, hot guy and hot gal. I'll lay you odds that they're makin' it already or have plans to do it very soon. I'm just sayin'."

The other three moaned and shook their heads.

"I'm just sayin', it'll happen. You heard it here first, folks. Shee-it."

## CHAPTER 53

**VICTORIA WAITED UNTIL THE CLINIC HAD CLOSED** at nine to let the students work with some of her clients. She split the four up into pairs, two to a room. Ronaldo Soto had apparently left long ago, so she would have to divide her time between the sessions. She and one pair of students would enter together and leave together after a half-hour. She would do the same with the other pair. If there was more to do, they would go back later.

† † †

The first client was Angelina Montez, a mother of three small children, whose boyfriend beat her repeatedly when he was out of jail. She sat down across from Victoria, who was behind her desk. Cecilia and Asa sat in chairs slightly behind her. From the start, Montez talked about her problems openly. It did not seem to matter that the other two were students. To her, they were all lawyers, and she needed their help. As she told her story, she stared at her hands, fingering a rosary the entire time.

"My Carlos used to be a good man," she began. "He worked regular, like in a garage as a mechanic. He knows cars and did fine for a year or so. His boss was good to him, and he got raises—more money to give to me. We have three kids—one older one I had by an old man who forced himself on me when I was cleaning his house. She is now ten. Carlos and I had sex the first night we met, and I got pregnant."

She looked up as if expecting some kind of reprimand.

"Go on, Angelina," said Victoria. "You are among friends."

"I had twins, you see, and a difficult time all along. I couldn't have sex during that time, so Carlos started being with other women. He didn't come home much and when he did, he was usually drunk." She pulled back her hair revealing a long scar on her forehead. "One night he cut me with a broken bottle," she explained, "and I got this as a souvenir."

"Were the twins born by then?" asked Victoria.

"Oh yeah, but fortunately, my mom had them that night," said Angelina.

"Did Carlos ever mistreat the kids?"

"No, never. He was bad but not **that** bad."

Cecilia raised her hand.

"Yes, Cecilia. Do you have a question?" asked Victoria.

"I wondered if you have thought about divorcing Carlos."

"Oh, *señorita,* we are not married," said Angelina.

※ ※ ※

After Angelina left the room, Victoria stepped out into the hall and motioned for Nathan and Alex to come in. "Come in, guys. I want all of you to hear from a new client."

"We'll be right with you, *señor*," she shouted to an older man sitting in the waiting room. She walked back down the hall to her office and returned with a young Hispanic woman.

"This is Ana Montoya."

The young woman smiled and nodded to the group.

"Please, sit down everyone," said Victoria.

They all sat down in the chairs around the long table.

"These are my interns: Cecilia, Asa, Nathan, and Alex. They attend the law school at UCLA and are interested in immigration."

Victoria turned to the others. "I want Ana to tell you her story, but before she does, I have a question for you all. What do you think of when you look at her? I mean, what do you see?"

Ana shifted nervously in her chair, obviously uncomfortable to be the center of attention in this way.

Victoria glanced at her. "I don't mean to put you on the spot, Ana. I have a reason for asking."

"Pretty girl," said Alex.

"Beautiful girl," said Asa.

"Smart girl," said Nathan.

"A young woman who looks like us, like a student," said Cecilia.

"Exactly," said Victoria. "Ana might well be sitting in a class next to you."

"And she isn't because she's illegal," said Alex, as always getting to the point, albeit abruptly.

"Ana, tell us about yourself," said Victoria, in a soft voice. "We are very interested."

Ana squared her shoulders and cleared her throat. "As you said, young *señor*, I am illegal in the eyes of the law. My parents came to this country when I was one year old. We paid a *coyote* to get us to Texas and the home of my aunt. We had to cross many rivers and face the dangers you read about—wild animals, bad men, people who tried to cheat us."

Victoria poured Ana a glass of water, and Ana went on to talk about the family's migration to Los Angeles, their hard work to establish a business and even buy a house, plus her years in Catholic school where she was an honor student, editor of the school newspaper, and valedictorian. The nuns at the school helped her get accepted at the local community college, where she excelled as well.

"And now you want to get into a university to finish your education," said Nathan, always precise in his thinking.

Ana nodded.

"Don't tell me, let me guess," said Asa, whose own life had been filled with setbacks. "You can't get in for some reason. Not grades, but maybe money?"

Victoria smiled at the perceptiveness of her interns.

"Yes, that's right," said Ana, nodding her head. "My parents can't afford to pay for university tuition, and because they are illegal—and I guess I am illegal too—they can't get a loan. My parents are afraid all the time that our status will be discovered. I don't know any other country but the United States. I do speak Spanish, but I know I could not get along in Mexico. It would be a strange country for me."

"But you could apply without any worries if the president's new legislation was approved," said Cecilia.

"I think so, yes," said Ana. "Right now, however, my parents are afraid for me to even apply for a scholarship. They worry that we might all be deported."

Victoria stood up. "Ana, it's getting late. I promise you that we will try to help you. Leave all of your paperwork with me, and we will review it."

The four students stood up and shook hands with Ana, both Cecilia and Alex sneaking in a hug.

"This is what we're facing," said Victoria, after Ana had left the room. "Dull statistics have a whole new meaning when you talk to people like Ana. We will try to help her, I promise you that."

She turned to Asa and Cecilia. "Now, will you two please step out and ask Mr. Sanchez to come in. Nathan, Alex, and I need to hear his story before we wind up this day."

Omar Sanchez was a distinguished-looking man about fifty who was dressed in a gray, double-breasted suit, a shirt and tie, with a matching handkerchief in the pocket of his coat. A closer look revealed frayed cuffs on both his pants and the shirt. But Nathan noticed that his shoes were shined and the lenses in his glasses were clean.

"*Señor* Sanchez," said Victoria, "it is good to meet you." She acknowledged the others with a wave of her hand. "My interns, Nathan and Alex."

"Good to meet you, sir," they both said in unison.

"Please tell us what we can do for you," said Victoria.

Without hesitation, Sanchez began to talk. "I was born in Juárez but was brought to this country by my parents when I was very young. My father started a business and became very successful. He imported Mexican art, which he sold in his own shop and to others who had shops. I went to college and started working in the store after I graduated. After about a year, I discovered that my father had borrowed money from the boss of a drug cartel, a *Señor* Ernesto Robles, to keep the doors open. He needed a cushion of cash to do that."

He stopped talking and looked at Victoria. "Could I have a glass of water?"

Nathan jumped up and filled a glass with water and handed it to Sanchez.

*"Muchas gracias,"* he said, then gulped it down.

"You were saying, *Señor* Sanchez," said Victoria.

"Oh, yes, pardon me, *señorita*. I get easily distracted with all this worry. My father could not pay, so I think they killed him."

"Who killed him?" asked Alex, without getting a nod from Victoria to speak.

"The gang. He was hit by a truck one night when he was going home."

"When was this?" asked Nathan.

"Ten years ago."

"TEN YEARS AGO!" all three of them exclaimed.

"And you're just telling someone about it now?" asked Victoria. "Did you go to the police?"

"Oh, no," he said. "I feared for my life and my mother's life, so I kept quiet. And I started paying back *Señor* Robles little by little."

"He accepted that?" she asked.

"Yes, he did. For a crook, he was a nice man."

"Sounds like a cool cat," said Alex with a smirk. "A real gentleman."

Victoria shook her head. "No editorial comments, please Alex."

"Sorry."

"So, if this arrangement was working well for you, why are you here today?" she asked.

"Because *Señor* Robles died last year, and the new guys in charge are not so nice. They came around to my shop and threatened me if I did not pay the whole amount."

Victoria thought for a moment. "I don't see that we can do anything for you, *Señor* Sanchez. Your only option is to go to the police. We offer legal advice, not any kind of protection. The law is the only protection we give here. What you are facing is extortion."

"Extortion? What's that?"

"It's where someone tries to make you do something you don't want to do by threatening you with bodily harm or blackmail."

"Oh, yes, I see," he said.

Victoria stood up.

"I am sorry we couldn't be of any help, *Señor* Sanchez."

"*Gracias, señorita.*"

"If you change your mind, I can give you the name of several policemen who handle this kind of thing."

"No *policío*," he said, fear in his eyes. "No *policío!*"

As they walked out the door of her office, Victoria heard a scream from the front of the building. She ran to the anteroom, followed by Alex and Nathan. The receptionist, Gloriana, was sobbing as she faced four men who were brandishing guns. *Señor* Sanchez disappeared out the back door.

Victoria put out her arms as if to shield the others from whatever was to come. "What is the meaning of this?" she said with as much courage as she could muster.

The men stepped aside so that a tall man, who appeared to be the boss, could walk by them. He had an imposing look at first, with his long coat and swagger and piercing eyes. But when she saw the tattoo of some kind of animal on his neck and face, Victoria knew she was in the presence of pure evil.

"You are very beautiful, *señorita*. I can see already that I am going to enjoy your company," he sneered as his men laughed. "But first, you need to take me to Lorenzo Madrid."

Victoria's eyes flashed in defiance. "I know of no such person," she said.

"*Señorita*, you disappoint me," he said, walking over to her. "I thought you were smart with your law degree and legal clinic and all. And this desire to help our people. Very nice. But you must not lie to me like that."

Then he slapped her in the face so hard that she bit her lip, and it started bleeding.

Alex ducked around the men and lunged at the big man. Seeing him out of the corner of his eye, the big man pulled a knife and thrust it at him. Alex dodged the direct hit, but the blade caught him in his face, and he fell to his knees, blood running down his face.

Victoria started to run back down the hall and yelled to the others, "RUN AS FAST AS YOU CAN! GET OUT OF HERE!"

The big man advanced on her and grabbed her by the hair. "You disappoint me again, *señorita*." Then he slapped her again and this time the blow knocked her out.

"Get them both out of my sight," Pantera said to his men. "I need to think."

He sat down on a dilapidated chair and pulled a flask out from one of the deep pockets of his coat. He took several deep gulps and wiped his mouth.

"I need to think."

## CHAPTER 54

**PEREZ WATCHED THIS SCENE UNFOLDING** from the shadows, letting Pantera handle the situation in his usual violent way—for now, at least. If his long experience as a gang leader had taught him nothing else, it was that you get more out of people by being reasonable—at least at first—than by scaring them and beating them.

He respected Victoria Ramos for protecting her friend, Lorenzo Madrid, even though he hated the man for what he had done to *Señor* Robles and still wanted to see him dead. That would come in good time. He had to admit that he was curious about Madrid, since he had been so successful in evading them. Of course, the men who had been looking for him were stupid, as was Pantera, their self-appointed leader.

The man's raving broke Perez's train of thought.

"Who is this woman?" Pantera was looking at Gloriana, Victoria's frightened receptionist.

His men shrugged their shoulders.

"Kill her!" he shouted.

One of Perez's men, either Nestor or Saul, rushed over to Perez and whispered in his ear.

"Wait, *Señor* Pantera," said Perez.

Pantera turned and glared at him with a "how dare you interrupt me" look on his face. *"Que pasa?"* He held up his hands, palms up.

"This woman is the sister-in-law of my man Saul. She tipped us off about Madrid coming here."

The man whispered something in Perez's ear again.

"Sorry. My mistake. She is my man Nestor's sister-in-law."

"What the fuck do I care whose sister-in-law she is!" snarled Pantera. "Get her out of here! And *señorita*, if I was you, I'd get me another job far away from this place. *Comprende?*"

Gloriana nodded her head quickly and ran out the front door.

By this time, Victoria was regaining consciousness and moaned softly. Alex was leaning against the wall nearby, holding a handkerchief on his wounded face.

"She needs help," said Perez, nodding toward Victoria.

"Yeah, sure, go ahead. What the hell. I don't want you to think that I am some kind of monster," said Pantera.

Perez knelt down and helped Victoria sit up. She began to rub her head. The blood from her cut lip had congealed and had stopped dripping.

"Miss Ramos," Perez said softly, as he started to massage her neck. "Can you hear me?"

"Of course, she can hear you," shouted Pantera. "I didn't hit her in the ear." For some reason, that struck Pantera as being funny, and he began to laugh loudly. As if on cue, his men joined in. Perez failed to see the humor in any of it.

"Enough of this!" Pantera shouted. "I need to see the others. I need to see what kind of..."

He turned to Felix, who suggested, "Power? Leverage?"

"What is 'leverage'? I do not know that word."

"The same as 'power,' *señor*," answered Felix.

"I like 'power' the best because I am very powerful. Right, *amigos?*"

The members of the gang all said at once, *"Sí, señor."*

"As I was saying, I need to see what kind of power I have over these punks. Where are they?"

Cecilia, Nathan, and Asa had been thrown in the conference room after they tried to escape. When Pantera entered, they stopped talking.

"Plotting your escape?" he asked, sneering. "You can't escape from the great Pantera. Like the jungle cat I am named for, I am everywhere and I see everything. Now, let's get loaded up—we are all going for a ride!"

Hearing this, Cecilia began to cry. Nathan and Asa were dry-eyed but looked grim.

## CHAPTER 55

**LORENZO MADE A CALL TO DETECTIVE BERMAN** as he sped along the 101 freeway to the 5 freeway to get to Boyle Heights. Unfortunately, it went to voicemail. Even though traffic was light at this early hour, it still took him forty-five minutes to get to the nursery.

From the street, the nursery grounds looked deserted. The small building that housed the retail shop was in the center of the yard. As he had seen on his earlier drive, it was in ruin. Windows were broken, doors were either gone or smashed in, and graffiti covered the walls. The plants that had not withered and died from neglect had grown to enormous heights.

Lorenzo parked on the street and crept along the side fence to the back of the property where his father had built a larger building which he turned into a greenhouse. There he had grown many of the plants he sold in the shop and stored the fertilizer and garden tools. It saddened Lorenzo to think that his homosexuality had brought ruin to his father, his mother, and this place. The fact that he couldn't help it was beside the point.

As he ducked through a hole in the chain-link fence, Lorenzo could see a group of people inside the building. As he got closer, he saw several Hispanic men standing in front of several other people sitting on the floor. Victoria was sitting there and so were Alex, Nathan, Cecilia, and Asa.

A tall man in a long coat was standing in front them. "Your precious teacher will be here soon, unless he has abandoned you," Pantera shouted. "That would not surprise me. Did you know he is a *maricón?* Do you know what that means in English?"

They all looked at him blankly—those who knew kept quiet.

"That means that he likes to fuck little boys." He sneered as he said that and began to laugh. Some of his other men joined in. "He has no interest in you, *Señorita* High-and-Mighty Ramos. But he might take a strong interest in the three of you." He looked at Nathan, Asa, and Alex and laughed again.

"We will wait for him a little bit more," continued Pantera. "But he probably won't be coming to save you."

"I wouldn't be so sure about that," said Lorenzo, as he stepped through a gaping hole in the wall and walked over to Pantera.

"We knew you'd come," said Asa. "We knew it!"

"Shut up, you little prick," hissed Pantera, then turned to Lorenzo. "So this is the great Lorenzo Madrid."

He walked over to Lorenzo and then around him, apparently sizing him up. "Not bad, not bad. Maybe too skinny. And maybe too brainy for his own good!"

He turned to one of his men. "Frisk him and make sure he has no weapons."

Right then, Lorenzo decided that this man was all bluff and swagger—cruel and remorseless but not really very smart. Best to keep him talking as long as possible.

"You know me, *señor*, but I do not know you," he said. "Who are you?"

"Aren't you the cool one," replied Pantera. "Trying to kill time? I will play your game. I am called Pantera. Do you know what that means?"

"I believe it translates to panther," answered Lorenzo.

"That is correct. You did not leave all your Spanish heritage behind when you became a white man."

Lorenzo's eyes flashed. "I will wager that..."

Pantera held up his hand and turned to the short, nervous young man standing near him. "What is 'wager'?"

"It is like a 'bet,'" he answered.

"You may continue," he said to Lorenzo.

"I will bet that I have done more for our people than you have ever thought of doing. You use them for your own purposes, you make money off them and turn them into killers, and all for what? For your glory and fame and to make you money. And what do you do with that money? I'll wager that you spend it on whores and booze and fancy cars and houses."

Pantera smiled, walked over to Lorenzo, and stood very close to him. "Are you finished?"

"I could go on, but you get my point, I think."

"I get your point, and now you will get mine."

Pantera stepped back and kicked Lorenzo in the testicles so hard that he fell to the floor in pain, almost blacking out.

As Lorenzo fell, both Asa and Nathan tried to reach him, but Pantera's men stopped them.

"Let him think this over for a while," Pantera said. "Now, I want to talk to you punks. I need to know you better, especially you, miss . . ." He turned to Cecilia.

"Don't tell him," shouted Asa. One of the men hit him.

"Cecilia Vega," she said, still crying.

"Come closer so I can see you better," said Pantera, sitting down on a broken chair.

She complied quickly. As she stood in front of him, Pantera started to unbutton her blouse.

"*Señor* Pantera, I think we need to finish our job here and get going," said Perez, who had been watching with growing agitation. This was no way to get his revenge against Madrid, and he wanted no part of this sideshow.

Pantera shoved Cecilia away from him, and she staggered back to where the others were standing.

"I hate to admit it," said Pantera, "but you are right. This is no time for fucking. I'll do that later with both *señoritas*." He smiled as he contemplated such a scene.

"Drag him over here," he said to his men, gesturing to Lorenzo, who was still lying on the floor. "We'll take care of him first."

## CHAPTER 56

**THE PAIN IN LORENZO'S LOWER REGIONS SUBSIDED** after a few minutes, but he stayed where he was to have more time to think. At this point, his only goal was to get Victoria and the students out of there to safety. How he would do this was the question.

This maniac Pantera obviously wanted him, and holding the others was the bait to get him there. And it had worked. But why was Pantera after him? His involvement in the death of Ernesto Robles, probably his former boss, had to be the reason. Although plausible, this theory lacked one key fact: given Pantera's personality, he wanted to be in charge. With Robles out of the way, he now **was** the boss, and he obviously loved that role. He was into swaggering and bullying, and loved to bend people to his will, using his gang of thugs and lots of guns to do that.

Lorenzo moaned and opened his eyes. He started to sit up, but one of the goons pushed him back.

"Let him up," said Pantera. "I want to hear what he has to say."

Lorenzo sat up and looked over at Victoria and the students. "I'm sorry," he mouthed.

"What did you say?" asked Pantera. "I will decide when you can speak to your friends!"

Should he be submissive or confrontational? Lorenzo pondered for a moment and then decided on his second choice.

"Let my friends go, Pantera!"

"I will decide when and if that happens," he said. "You seem to forget who is in charge here."

Lorenzo glanced at the other man—Perez, he thought he'd heard someone call him. He was observing everything but not becoming involved. How did he accept Pantera as a leader? How did he feel about Pantera's unpredictability? Although obviously a bad guy himself, he might just be a more intelligent bad guy. Lorenzo had to find out.

"*Señor* Perez, you do not strike me as a stupid man. My death would be easy to pull off. I am single, living here temporarily and from another state. But the murders of five other people, all local, all with families who would demand answers. And Miss Ramos and her clinic are very important to the community here. Lots of questions if anything happens to her, right?"

Perez looked at him but did not answer.

Pantera was not amused that Lorenzo was directing his comments at someone other than him. He walked over to Lorenzo and grabbed him by the shoulders.

"Look, *amigo*, you will talk only to me!" he shouted. "I am *el jefe* here, and I give the orders. Perez works for me! You would do well to remember that! *Comprende?*"

"Oh, I won't forget it, *señor*," said Lorenzo. "And may I make a simple request?"

"A request from a soon-to-be dead man?" Pantera contemplated his fingernails before answering. "Of course, I am not totally without..." He turned to Felix.

"Compassion?"

"Yes, yes, I knew that."

He looked back at Lorenzo. "What do you want?"

"I wondered if you could brush your teeth or eat a breath mint," said Lorenzo, straight-faced. "You've got really bad breath."

Pantera looked stunned that anyone would have the guts to talk to him like this. He started to hit Lorenzo again but held back at the last minute.

"I think you are deliberately trying to make me angry to distract me, *Señor* Madrid. Very smart, or so you think. But I will not let that happen." He turned to his two men, ignoring Saul and Nestor. "I am too smart for that, right *amigos?*"

They nodded, but Perez's men did not.

"I repeat, let them go," said Lorenzo. "You've got me now, and that is what you've wanted all along."

"Yes, you are right," said Pantera. "You are the focus for all of us. I have to admit, though, that I did not even know anything about you until my man, Esteban, here, told me that you had killed our beloved *Señor* Robles."

Lorenzo turned to Perez, who seemed to stiffen a bit at being called "my man" by Pantera. "Were you there?"

Perez shook his head. "No, but I know you called in the DEA and then Robles was soon dead—out there in the Oregon desert, far from home, far from his men. He was like a father to me."

Now, the whole thing was becoming clear to Lorenzo.

"So that's what this is all about. But you are going to punish me for something I did not do. I was being held by Robles because he thought I broke up his drug operation. His man Paco shot him just before the DEA got there. It will be in the report. I think I can get you a copy."

Perez waved his hands dismissively. "You're making this up. I don't believe you."

Lorenzo shrugged. "Okay, but it's the truth. After Robles was killed, it didn't take long for the DEA to shut down your whole Northwest operation."

"Don't I know," said Perez. "The DEA shut it down, and it has taken me a long time to set it back up."

Lorenzo smiled and looked at Pantera. "And then *Señor* Pantera sweeps in and takes over."

Perez's head moved in an almost imperceptible nod, but he said nothing.

"You know nothing of our business affairs, Madrid," said Pantera, becoming agitated. "You are trying to distract us from the business at hand."

Lorenzo nodded. "You are very smart, *Señor* Pantera. I can't outguess you. I realize that now."

Pantera smiled, apparently pleased that Lorenzo was finally understanding how intelligent he was.

"A word, *Señor* Pantera?" asked Perez.

"Now what do you want? Everyone seems to want to distract me."

The two walked to the other end of the room. Although Lorenzo could not hear what was being said, he could tell by their gestures that Perez was trying to convince Pantera to do something he did not want to do. After five minutes, Pantera walked back to the center of the room and talked to the five hostages who were sitting on the floor.

"My man Perez has convinced me to take you outside so you do not have to witness what is going to happen to your beloved teacher," he said. "I am a . . ." He turned to Felix.

"Compassionate?"

"Yes, of course. I knew that! I am a compassionate man, as I said before."

"Let me assist you," said Perez. He walked over to Saul and Nestor and talked to them in low tones. Then loudly, no doubt for Pantera's benefit, he said, "Take these people over to the other building."

While they were being herded away, Victoria broke free and ran to Lorenzo. "You are a brave man, Lorenzo. I am proud to have known you."

"We will never forget you," said Asa.

"You got THAT right," Alex chimed in.

"Most impressive," said Nathan.

And Cecilia just cried harder.

"Isn't this a touching scene," said Pantera. "Don't cry for me, *Señor* Lorenzo. I loved that musical about the great Eva Perón." He paused to remember it. "Ha, ha. Now I am a composer of great music!"

He turned to his men. "Get them out of here!"

They were all pushed outside, leaving Lorenzo alone with Pantera and Perez. Even Felix left the room.

Pantera had a strange look on his face when he said, "You know, Perez, you didn't know your sister very well. She was ashamed of you and did not want to see you again because of what you have become—a petty drug dealer."

Perez's eyes flashed. "What are you saying?" he asked.

Pantera smiled knowingly. "Let's just say that I knew her even better than you did. But you know she was dishonoring you and all of us with her behavior, so I had that taken care of."

Lorenzo could see that it was taking all the self-control Perez could muster not to jump at Pantera and strangle him.

Then it all became clear to him: Margarita Askew was Perez's sister! And it was Pantera who had her shot—maybe as a means of controlling Perez, thought Lorenzo. Who could understand this madman's thought processes? Lorenzo had suspected that the killer had been one of her former lovers, and it sounds like he was. With that mystery solved, Lorenzo could now capitalize on the rising tension between his two captors to try to escape.

"I want to tell you how sorry I was to learn of your sister's death," Lorenzo said to Perez.

Perez looked surprised. "What do you know of my sister?"

"I am teaching at the law school this semester, and I met her on several occasions at the dean's . . . I should say, her house. She was a wonderful lady." Lorenzo decided that a lie might serve his purposes better here than the truth about that wretched woman.

"I had not been in touch with her much in recent years," said Perez, shaking his head as if regretting not being in contact with her.

"That's enough!" shouted Pantera, obviously losing patience. "We have business to finish here!"

"Before you do what you are going to do to me," said Lorenzo, "I want to know who you are and where you came from. I know

Perez's motivation, but what is yours? Are you just following his lead because you are now his boss?"

Perez's eyes flashed at the use of that word. Lorenzo sensed that he did not like his descent into the lower ranks of the organization.

"You don't remember me, do you?" said Pantera.

Lorenzo shook his head.

"I remember you. I was surprised when I saw your picture."

Lorenzo looked confused. "I am certain I've never met you. Believe me, I would remember."

Perez looked confused, but said nothing.

"It is like our destinies are wrapped together," continued Pantera.

"What are you talking about?" asked Lorenzo.

"I know I look different from the last time you saw me. It was many years ago, and I have changed. I am taller and more muscular and have added these tattoos to signify my high status in the cartel."

Both Perez and Lorenzo listened intently.

"I got my first tattoo, here under my eye, after my first kill." He pointed to his face and the tiny tattoo that looked like a tear. "Not a tear of sadness but a tear of joy. You know who my first kill was?"

"I have no idea," said Lorenzo, "but I'm sure you will tell me."

"It happened in your father's nursery."

Lorenzo blinked in disbelief. "You are Eduardo?"

"The very same, *maricón!* And my first kill was your lover, I think Scott was his name. Another *maricón*, another queer like you!"

Lorenzo lunged at Pantera, but Perez deflected him, and he fell to his knees.

"You bastard! You murderer! You ruined my life!" he shouted.

Pantera sneered. "And what do you think happened to my life? I was arrested on suspicion of killing your boyfriend, but I was a juvenile so they could not prosecute me as an adult. I was deported instead. My parents tried to help me, but they had no papers, and they were deported too. I had never been to Mexico and did not even speak Spanish very well. But there I was, right in the middle of some remote village. My parents had no money; my father could not get a job. It killed them, and all because of you and your precious boyfriend."

"I'm sorry for what happened to your family, but you were a murderer," shouted Lorenzo. "You are still a murderer. You deserved what happened to you!"

"And you deserve what is going to happen to you!" said Pantera, his voice rising. "What you are, a *maricón*, is a disgrace to our country, a disgrace to our Mexican cultural heritage."

"That's a laugh, Pantera! Do you not know that our male ancestors had sex with other men and boys throughout history? And why is that worse than you and your use of whores? You would love to rape Victoria and Cecilia right now and would have done so if Perez here hadn't stopped you. You are a predator of another kind. I am not a predator. I just happened to love another man, and why is that so bad?"

Pantera waved his hand in dismissal. "I am tired of all this talk. Shoot him, Perez, so we can get on with our business."

Lorenzo closed his eyes and wondered if there would be much pain and how long before death would come.

Perez pulled his gun and cocked it, then aimed it at Lorenzo. He pulled the trigger.

A loud roar reverberated through Lorenzo's skull. Then he heard a loud thump, as if someone had fallen.

He opened his eyes to see Pantera lying dead on the floor, blood running out of a hole in his head—right through the eye of his tattooed panther.

As Lorenzo waited for the next bullet to hit him, Perez lowered his gun and motioned with it toward the hole in the wall of the warehouse.

Stunned but with no hesitation, Lorenzo ran outside without looking back.

**THE END**